LAST TRAIN OUT

R. Boes

iUniverse, Inc.
New York Bloomington

LAST TRAIN OUT

iUniverse books may be ordered through booksellers or by contacting:

iUniverse
1663 Liberty Drive
Bloomington, IN 47403
www.iuniverse.com
1-800-Authors (1-800-288-4677)

ISBN: 978-1-4401-0014-7 (pbk)
ISBN: 978-1-4401-0013-0 (ebk)

Printed in the United States of America

iUniverse Rev. 10/21/08

*　*　*

For my sister Shay, my best friend growing up. So pure, my poor, sick, beautiful sister, Shay Full of Grace.

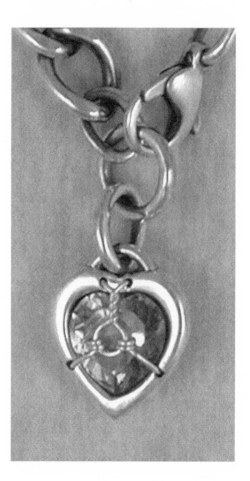

Chapter 1

3rd car from the rear

"Vanity of Vanities," says the Preacher, "Vanity of Vanities!
All is Vanity." Eccl. 1:2

*   *   *

Above the line nothing is futile. No mirrors, only black glass, ink and page. She was a working girl who always slept with a light on. The lamp burning at her work bench shown through the crack in her bedroom door, a beam of light like a lighthouse lantern beckoning out across a sea of fear and darkness, resting at the foot of her comforter. "This way I don't have to grope around in the dark if I wake up with a bright idea, hungry, a bad dream, or I gotta pee."

*   *   *

3:00 AM some 30 years later. Can't sleep, can't stop thinking about Jess. I've survived that last book. The images in the glass are only ghosts; I'm trying not to look. I only want to cry. Bury my head in the page. It's just me and this coffee cup, another sip, puff, guttural cough. All these holes, buttons and bullets, across my chest, up and down my arms, blood everywhere. (pause) She was always working, busy, busy, busy, never slept much, sometimes she'd forget to eat. Always thinking, doing, she never knew the date or time, sometimes she didn't know what day of the week it was. Saturday was Sunday, Monday like any other day of the week. "Work was work," she'd say, "8 days a week." Some days she made me angry, joyful, sad, but she always made me laugh. She almost never ate lunch. We'd spend only a year together, years ago, madly in love, but only a sketch, a formidable start, charcoaled, crude, but penciled in truth. And the first lines of a lover's portrait cycle agelessly eternal like Vermeer. Still, I wouldn't know that much about her until 30 years later.

The baby wrens in my blue birdhouse aren't awake yet. God, it's just me, you, those crickets, and memories of Jess. I'm out of cigarettes, 4 hours till the smoke shop opens. I'm out of bread, milk, pretzels, all but the scrapings of a peanut butter jar. My house is in order, inside I'm a disaster. "Pristine," she'd call me, which was better than asshole. She'd toss the cushions from the couch, storm into the bedroom and mess up my sock drawer, pull the sheets from the bed.

"Jess!"

Today's her 51st birthday, would be, but she's dead! Jessica died 3 weeks ago. Her parents called the super, she hadn't shown up for her cousin's baby christening the day before, didn't answer the phone. Harold found her on the living room floor, a large, almost-empty bottle of Listerine on the coffee table, two empty mouthwash bottles at her work bench, its lamp still burning. Harold said, "No smell of death, couldn't have been there long. Dressed, place was clean. She looked real good for a dead person." Yeah, she always looked good.

*   *   *

That cough made me dizzy. Above the line we are all of service, all good soldiers. I am like a tree, words for leaves. I can write through the tears. Branches reaching, infant-like fingers, no moon or stars, but for a big thick slice of black heavenly pie. (pause) Is Jess in heaven making fine jewelry for God? I never wear the stuff; it has no real purpose, means of survival. Yeah, I did open a sterno can with a cross once. Years ago Jess made me a key chain, it broke.

You stone believers, idle worshipers, graven souls who only want to live forever. Eternity in a handbasket, a walk to Grandma's, an Emerald City. Religiously grinding gears, kneeling in pews, falling prey to wolves. Afraid of nothing, of dying, that being dead is nowhere. Jess, she was no Little Red Riding Hood; I'm no bald angry man behind the curtain.

A mountain view of the Promised Land just out of reach. A train whistles off in the distance, down by the river, grows further away with each passing year. I only hear it anymore in these early hours of morning before the clatter of business. A refreshing clear stream, greener pastures like when I was Little Boy Blue.

I'm older now but still that boy, still hitting homers over the fence, flattening pennies on the rails. Walking the track like a tightrope line, the high-wire at the Big Top, a hundred feet above a cheering crowd. I love that train whistle like the soft play of wind chimes off the back deck. Dad's coming home from work. It's Christmas Eve; tonight we're off to Grandma and Pop Pop's house. Over the bridge, above the line, the splendor of city lights. We'll sing Christmas carols to the toll collectors, "We wish you a merry Christmas, we wish you a merry Christmas, we wish you a merry Christmas, and a happy New Year." We'll all laugh together.

There'll be so many presents under the tree. My big cousin Lois will help me and Shay read the tags; the biggest ones were always for us. She'd share in our excitement; help us wait patiently for gifts to be opened. One year Pop Pop did the tree all up in red, red bulbs, red lights, red tinsel. He was the first to die, they're all gone now. My aunts, uncles, Cousin Jack.

I'm an empty vacant flat car, hauling nothin', 3rd car from the rear. I don't know the old man in the glass. He don't care if his hair's not combed, he's just looking for that little thing that hides itself below his fat belly, hadn't seen it in weeks like he was 5 months pregnant, and to boot his ass is falling off. Jess always said, "Guys in the gut, girls in the butt." I've got both sides failing.

This cup of coffee needs a cigarette. Think I've just started my next book. This must be it. Yeah, I'd survived the last one, that War, the streets, the drugs, the memory, my thoughts. I'd surrendered, won and lost, survived the sweats, nightmares, screams, bullets, shrapnel, kidney failure, cancer, surgery. I'd survived murder! That cough rattles my brain. Again I've survived the night.

Waiting. (pause) I'm waiting on the birds like angels, like words to circle my head like black-capped chickadees, the sweet song of flight. If! If they find me here I'll be complete, whole again, above the line like one, one branch of blue sky. I am of service. A soldier boy tryin' to be good. Again I will make the bed like Job on a good day, because, because I know nothing of the wonders of creation. A rhinoceros laughs hysterically while vultures clean its flesh from the earth. A red-breasted nut hatch, who I'd like to be, climbs down the side brick. All is vanity, vanity of vanities.

*　　　　*　　　　*

It was the fall of 72, my second year of college, the first day of writing class when I first saw Jessica. She walked in late in total disarray, dropping books, her red hair afire like a lioness through hoops of flame, like a tall sail ship coming into port, like a long sleek silver train. She was 5 foot 7, all of 108 pounds with a high booty like a prize colt, her curly mane flowing down around her waist. Her big green eyes like heaven's gate full of wonderment, intrigue. Her entire being brought forth empathy and applause. I was smitten with love. She was the most beautiful thing I'd seen since coming back from War. She rejuvenated my hopes and dreams; life was good again, worth living. She was something to live for. She seemed smart, strong, outspoken, asked and answered questions with authority. I sat in my corner, my perch like a red tailed hawk, watching, listening, her gracefulness like a liquid blue sky on a sea of fire and ice. She had more jewels than the Queen of Sheba, bracelets, earrings, rings, and chains glistened in the sun's ray, creating bands of light with every movement of her body and hands. She'd put Cleopatra to shame. What sold me, solidified my dreams like a soldier's last prayer were them muddy construction boots. (later) I was sitting in the commons, a soft easy chair, reading Blake's *The Marriage of Heaven and Hell*. She and a girlfriend walked past. She'd changed into a skirt, but kept them boots. Attempting to pull her sweater off, over her head, she'd lifted up her t-shirt. *Nice tits*, I thought, smiled and said, "You got skinny legs." Her girlfriend quickly tugged her t-shirt down. Jess looked me right in the eye, right through me, smiled, "I bet you got a skinny dick." The guy in the chair next to me, who I didn't know, started laughing, couldn't stop. Jess walked off. We'd spoken. God, I'd never been so happy, felt this good.

*   *   *

All cleaned up, the trash is out. I've got a drag strip in my throat. Seems the ashtray is smoking itself. It's a dead afternoon. (pause) I'm dead all over, stricken as if by the cold hand of God. I've got winter in my bones. A cup of hot tea to soothe my throat. An old postcard, a blue house, only wish I was there. Not a good day for words, not a good day for anything. Do I want to tell you this? Do I want to put myself through it? Do I have a choice? Does it matter? Does it matter if it doesn't matter? I'm trying not to smoke the next cigarette, but it doesn't matter. You're the only one I've left to talk with, and you don't have to listen. It doesn't matter. I don't care. That last book was all I really had to say. This here now is overtime, a second tour like working a double shift.

There's a beautiful sunset just over that hill, but I can't move. Jess, she'd convince me, but I'm stuck here writing this. No one calls, my sadness overwhelms them. Music plays soft, slow, a lone mourning dove takes flight. This time of day everything's leaving, the glass goes black, ghosts appear. I'd like to crawl up into a bullet cap and blast it all into oblivion.

I'm waiting on a still small package; get me out from myself, the memory, the bog. Soon I'll be taking my best shot, shoot blood on the ceiling, shred, shredding sheets of toilet paper like dead flesh scattered all about me. It won't mean nothin', I'll be unaffected, the crown Prince of Flight. (pause) Again the ashtray is clear; all the world is made of glass.

Went to the morning meeting the other day, hadn't been there since Jess died. She'd stopped going there months ago; she'd been propositioned by the Big Man, Mr. AA. I've known a handful of women over the years who this fat, sad fuck has offered to spank. "It'll help you with your anger issues." He's even spanked a few. He preys on really sick, emotionally disturbed newcomers, Mr. Big with his 20 years of expertise. He's a braggart, a bully. Wants to be anything other than who he is, Mr. Nobody who sells cleaning products to the industrial complex. He's a wannabe, wants to be a black blues musician, a wise guy, an ex con, a gun slinger.

When I first moved to the area 9 years ago, he caught wind I'd been in Vietnam, he'd read all the War books. "Hey, you were with the Cav, kick ass unit, man." He knew the entire lingo but didn't have a fucking clue, possessed all the bravado of being out of range. He'd get drunk in bars, tell people he was a War hero. What kind of sad sack wants to be the hero of a lost War, a War that should have never been fought?

Mr. Big, 6 foot, 280, is a smart man, frustrated, should have stayed in school, a tormented victim, a martyr for a wife and two children he must provide for, who don't even like 'im. Two or 3 meetings a day just to get out of the house. (pause) Wish my package would get here. The Big Man pretends to know it all, talks down to everyone, gives a history lesson every time he speaks like he was there with Bill and Bob, helped write the Big Book (AA's general text), he's mostly full of shit. He boasts about taking out the trash, all the service he does, all the people he's helped. How about all the women you've estranged from this meeting? Still, I do feel sorry for him.

A nice cup of coffee. Blue jay squawking in the distance, no, not quite the shriek of a blackbird, not so piercing, not a gaping wound. (pause) I need to hit the bank, splash some water on my face. (pause) Still, I come back orange. Some music. Another page, another day without Jess. Yeah, we were the best of friends.

Can't go to that meeting, don't trust myself. (pause) Another cup. Opened all the windows. I'm up at a reasonable hour like a normal person; don't have to look at myself in the black glass. No, I don't need an assault charge, could break a chair over his fucking head if he gets in my face.

A few years back I'd had my fill of someone who'd disrespected me once too often. Blindsided 'im, knocked him over a table flat on his ass, got my hands around his neck, started strangling 'im, screaming at him. "I've had enough of you motherfucker!" He was turning blue, blue like a block of wood. Bob and the Big Man were the only two in the room, the meeting hadn't started yet. "Let 'im up, let 'im up!" Bob kept saying it, saying it over, and again. I was gonna let Joe up, but just not yet. Mr. Big said, did nothing. I wasn't having a flashback, knew who I was choking, wasn't gonna kill 'im, just wanted a deeper shade of blue. Bob pulled me off. Joe has never disrespected me again; he's courteous these days, polite. A few days later a rumor was circulating; the Big Man had broken it up, saved Joe's life. I don't need to guess who propagated that bullshit.

I'll have one more cup, make the bed. I'll go see Robby, my good friend, book agent, who lives around the corner. Sold off the last of the royalties on my last book, keeping 51 percent, I'm in the black. (pause) The bed's made. Jess's daughter Maria now gets her 4 percent. It's a nice day out there despite my mood. Monty, Robby's cat who likes to butt heads walks past, on the prowl, was born to hunt. Need to take care of some business stuff, make a few phone calls. Need to rehearse a reading I've got coming up. This song is about being in the arms of an angel. Don't know where my angels are these days; I'm only filling up pages. You see, my halo's round my boot heels. Sure could use some good news, are there no babies being born, no bridegrooms? I sent off a copy of my last book to Tim O'Brien, no response. Know of only one bookstore in the world that has it on the shelf. (pause) The coffee pot's rinsed. (later) All my bills are paid; it feels good to be in the black, on the page. One phone message like a second wind, a distant shot at redemption. Above the line nothing drips, gutters, drainpipes, no water, wine, blood, or mouthwash. No need to repaint your house blue.

*   *   *

I was at the meeting, thought I'd say nothing but I was coming undone. I was sitting next to Romulus, he sensed my anxiety, stroked my back like a good friend. I got my hand up, had to say somethin' like I'd burst into flames if I didn't. Mr. Big was sitting across from me, on the other side of the rectangular group of tables we sit around. He'd already made his boast, all his thankless service, how the Washingtonians were bought and sold on the issue of slavery. Again what you must do and nothing really about himself. Again about all the people he'd helped. It was my turn now.

I need another cup, (pause) keep moving. Without pointing a finger, calmly, I said my mind. "There's a sick, sick pervert among us who preys on vulnerable, shaky, emotionally ill women, offers to spank 'em, help them with their anger issues. Chases 'em out of the room." The Big Man turned white, green, then red. "It's unacceptable, too many of you know about it, and just let it continue. Maybe, probably not, but just maybe Jess would have walked round the corner, come to this meeting. If! If she felt safe." Mr. Big squirmed in his seat, wriggled his fat ass in the chair until his chair broke, and landed him flat out on the floor! God was on my side, had brought the room's attention squarely where it belonged like a giant finger pointing at him. The sicker ones couldn't help but laugh, me too.

The ashtray is full. (pause) I'm more tired than awake. It's a hot afternoon, the kind that makes you wanna lay up and do nothing. I left the meeting before it ended, upset; two people followed me out. Richard shook my hand, Claudia thanked me, "Somebody needed to do that, it took a lot of courage."

"Is that why you didn't?" The Big Man had spanked one of her sponsees.

I walked myself home. It was a clear, subdued sky, more gray than blue like someone trying to speak who can't find the words. I walked the cracks of an eroding sidewalk, weeds stuck up, felt the pangs in my flat feet. And the sky broke over the mountain, light shot through like the Holy Ghost had lit me full of grace. "I did it for you baby," and I started to cry. (later) Haven't stopped crying since. Another cup. Tired, but don't wanna mess up the bed. The wind chimes 3 beats like a butterfly might circle one's soul before dying. Harold said, "It didn't look like a suicide, there wasn't any note."

Saw Jess's dad the other day, he and Mildred were cleaning out the apartment. Carried a box to the car. "She just couldn't get out from under." Never liked Jack much, even less these days, but couldn't help giving him a hug.

No one's saying how she died, mum on any autopsy, coroner's findings, the country club elite would be aghast. Sure it was alcohol poisoning, but were drugs involved? Jess never mentioned any suicidal ideation, she so loved Maria. Drugs weren't her thing. She'd been sober almost a year. What happened? (pause) The sun is disappearing; the glass is going black. How many more bullet holes before I stop shooting myself? I'll brush my 6 remaining teeth.

*   *   *

Lost a day. Another mess to clean up, both inside and out. And the wind chimes. I'm not really here, just these ghosts on a flat screen, looking back at myself. The birds and the sky are an hour away. The computer Robby gave me won't type the letter j, it's strange, I can't write her name. I need another cup of you. This cough is greater than who I'll ever be. (pause) Could do the morning meeting, I need a meeting, but don't need to see the Big Man ever again. I'm toying with a rock in my left hand, a small smooth stone Jess gave me, its broad even surface fits my thumb perfectly like a footprint on the brain; it's soothing, eases the bad with a good memory. Once was a key chain. I need to splash some water on my face, wake the fuck up. (pause) Ended the life of some crawly thing working its way across the kitchen floor. All is nothing. My reading's two days from here. 20 past 5, need a shave, a shower, all that goes with it. Need some hand lotion on my hands, arms, wrists. It's much too warm. Need ink. Milk. The letter j.

Where's my train whistle? (pause) Emptied the bathroom trash into a tall lemon-scented kitchen bag, and tossed it. All my guns are in the dumpster. Cough, more coughing. Harold the super, he reminds me of Harold the milkman. I'd ride with him on snowy days when school was cancelled. I'd sit on a milk crate; his truck had only a driver's seat. I'd run up your walk, steps, put bottles of milk in your milk box. Yeah, you don't see any boxes or milk trucks anymore. The snow ain't so deep these days. People started buying their own milk in stores like Garden State, Stewarts, Harold became a school crossing guard. On snowy mornings he'd hit me from behind with a snowball. He was a nice man, a lot like Harold the super, jovial, kind, good, a lot like Pop Pop. It's too bad Harold had to find Jess the way he did.

Again I've filled the page with nothing. The War never stops, lets me forget unlike Shay who can't remember anything. (pause) I barley survived last night, legs locked, knees swelled up like red balloons, stuck, frozen, standing in one place. Shred, shredding sheets of toilet tissue on a sea of black glass, dead flesh scattered all about me. I'd almost drowned. The bathroom looked like a battlefield, a slaughterhouse, blood on the floor, walls, and ceiling. The stench of death, that rotting taste in my mouth. They would have found me there, needles (guns) everywhere, looking back, petrified like Lot's wife in an upright position. Should have been a milkman.

I was scared to ask Jess on a date, fearful she'd reject me. (pause) Straightened a few pictures on the wall. "There was a crooked man, and he went a crooked mile." Guess I never felt good enough, not like Shay who was more than good. (pause) Jess deserved better than me, a ghostly man, a boyish soldier, stuck in a meaningless War. Couldn't free myself up. (pause) In those early days I said nothin', nothing of what I'd seen and done. I was afraid people wouldn't like me. Never said much to Jess about it, she didn't know, not until she read my book 30 years later. (pause) The bed's made. The bathroom smells like dead fish, rotting corpses strung up in the market place, it's what we did to prisoners if they didn't talk. God, I can't seem to get the blood out. Broke out a new razor, cut myself, washed my hair, brushed all my teeth. There are no dishes in the sink. I've got aloe on my wounds. 3rd car from the rear, vacant and flat. This just might be my finial uncoupling. My patio loveseat is made of tree branches by American Indians.

"Coo, coo." (pause)

"Coo," a lone mourning dove cooing back at me. It feels at home here, but oh so lonely, like how I miss my friend.

I'll do the meeting, can leave if I feel uncomfortable. Took my pills, one from each of 6 bottles worth, two shots off my inhaler. The mess has been contained; still I'm failing, falling through the cracks like lines of pavement, stuck to the page. It looks like rain, this sadness welling up inside me. The flower in the jar, the tiny kitchen table vase, is dead. I've lost my chariot, it's been repossessed, my fiery angel. Who will walk with me to the meeting?

Just to fill the page. If! Knowing I'll never be home free. The wind chimes. Guess I'm not alone here. (still morning) Something of a nap. Did the 7:30 AM meeting. Got milk. It was a good meeting. I'm feeling grateful, the Big Man was absent. I do, do believe. If! If only for my dying will stop the noise. Don't expect to finish this book, its okay, I already know how it ends. I'm one up on you. Truly, truly I believe I will be missed.

My mom called, she and my dad were married 60 years last month. She sounds her age, I'm sad. Still, I'd like to leave before they do, as selfish as that sounds, what with the War and Jess I've had my fill, couldn't bear losing them. She thought I had a cold, "Your voice sounds thick." I coughed a resonating cough from the bowels of my existence. "God, bless you!"

"That was a cough,"

"Oh."

"My voice is getting thicker-rah."

"What?"

"Thicker-rah!" She laughed, we laughed.

My throat is a patch quilt; I've got a 6-inch surgical scar on my neck as proof. Tuesday it's back to the cancer doctor. They'll take that little camera on a string, go up my nose and down my throat, make me gag. "Puff out your cheeks, relax, breath through your nose." It's been 9 months since my surgery, they never found the primary, but the cancer hasn't come back. Can't help thinking it will. I attended a group when I was first diagnosed, there were 5 others with the same type of cancer, two have died since, and another is terminal. (pause) Called Sam, he's the terminal one, he's a playwright, invited 'im to my reading, wanna give him a copy of my book.

This last song has no words. Again the ashtray is starting over. Nothing's clear that hasn't been soiled, the truth is in the water, all glass is vanity but for black glass. (pause) Called Larry, a fellow vet, author, our books were in the same review, that's how we met. He works at a rehab, a psych center; maybe he can get me some help. Left a vague message, nothing incriminating. I don't think it'll fix me, but it might buy me some time. I do need to survive my parents.

Me and Bukowski are school boys, yeah; we'd both like to carry your books. I know real good how to duck, cover up, live in a bunker, suck up mud, and go quietly into the night. I needed to get up the courage to ask Jess out, not doing so was eating me up inside. I felt sick to my stomach. I'll have one more cup. (pause) Paid the cable bill, it's all that came in the mail. No phone calls. "Nothing any good ever comes in the mail." Think she was right. I need a cough drop.

Another page. Heard she liked Beckett. Got tickets for an off-off-off -Broadway production of *Waiting for Godot*. I'm weavin' and bobbin' in and out of story like Muhammad Ali, my words are pretty. Need to do some laundry. I can fly like a butterfly, like a bullet, sting like a bee, split a tree. I'm above the line, and the music stops. Again I'm waiting on a still small package. "Be still, and know that I am God." It's written in the bigger than Big Book.

I'd finally got up the nerve, stopped her in the hallway, she was in a rush, always rushing. Made me nervous. I stumbled over my first few words, put too many off, offs before Broadway. Made her laugh. She corrected me, smiled and said, "Yes." Yes! Yes! Yes! Most of you wouldn't think of her as beautiful as I did, she was exquisite! I walked off down the hall, my feet elevated, off, off, off the ground. Out from the trenches. (pause) Maybe I can eat something now.

The ashtray is clean, clear glass, the coffee pot rinsed. Again the bed is made. I'm only waiting on a still small package. Shay Full of Grace is living her life out in a nursing home, has MS, had it some 20 years now, the progressive type. For some it just affects the body, but besides her physical limitations, her short-term memory is shot. She's stuck in bed anymore, wearing a diaper. Shay can feed herself but very, very slowly. We'd already be eating desert. She liked the movie she saw last night, "What was the title?" She forgot. "What was it about Mom?" She can't remember. "Who was in it?"

"Fuck you!" She tells her daughter Kate in a joking way. We all laugh at the jokes, there ain't nothin' else to do about it. Mom says, "She'd be so happy." But Shay forgets that her daughter Keri is pregnant with her first grandchild. Shay was born full of grace, was a nurse before she got sick, never smoked, drank, did any drugs. Never cared too much about herself, and everything she did was about helping people. She was a virgin when she got married, but her two girls weren't immaculately conceived. Now she just lies there all day and soils herself. "Where does this come from?" She always asks of me, "From hell! Life ain't fair!"

It's a good day for words. (later) It's a good day for small things, this broken keychain, this rock, a tiny blue postcard of a house. If! It was the little things that made me and Shay best of friends. How I'd sneak a shoe under her pillow, kill spiders in her bedroom. We'd always be there for each other. That time the neighborhood bully pushed me into the sticker bushes, "You leave my brother alone!" She punched, kicked and spit at him. I clocked him with a hard right when he wasn't lookin', knocked 'im cold. A year behind me in school, nobody messed with my kid sister. The only time she ever got mad at me was when I broke a gallon of Garden State milk in the back seat of her VW Bug, "That smell!" I scrubbed with everything but couldn't get it out. Her real name's Janice, but she's always been Shay. No one knows how or why I called her that, it's a mystery. I'd only just started talkin', maybe I couldn't say Janice, maybe I liked Shay better. A popular song on the radio went something like, *I don't want a ricochet romance, I don't want a ricochet love.* Maybe she was the Shay to my Rick.

All I'm doing here is filling the page. These were all good days, before the War, before Shay got sick. I need to give her a call. (pause) "Hey, you the girl they named that stadium after?" Made her laugh. Reminded her she'll be a grandmother soon.

Shay doesn't say much these days, "Yeah, just laying here. Nothin'. No visitors."

"I know Mom was there an hour ago."

"Oh, okay." She'll forget this phone call minutes after I hang up.

"From hell! Life ain't fair!" (pause)

Thunder and rain, sky flashing, listening to the sweet rasp of Janis. The condition of music, art without any glass. What's the truth anymore? I'm nothin', nothing but a scribe, unseen like the wind, a prayer, like the roots of a tree and how it moves from earth to sky, into one blue branch. Everything answers to the wind. I am poor of spirit, humble before the page. (pause) My pen runs out of ink. My bones unto dust; fire, air, and water will consume me. You will breathe me in like sky. This last song has no words.

*   *   *

It's raining, it's pouring, Jill is gone and Jack fills his bucket. The old man is snoring, no need to climb that hill again. Cat bird is calling, a soft purr like fish for the kettle. Lost a day, slept it off. The back wood is coming into view. This pen works fine, a fine black point. I'm not really here, but a memory, missing my Jill. Don't have the strength to do another shot; I'm on the backside of the page.

Above the line. Two butts in the ashtray. Need another cup. (pause) My hair's sticking up and out, I've got mine fields on the brain, smell of blood and rotting flesh. Jill kicks the bucket, and Jack fills the page. All is vanity. I need to do some laundry, need my black shirt for the reading tonight. Need to transfer these notes into a computer that types the letter j. Keep moving, tell the story.

Our first date. Terrific, great! (pause) She looked amazing, so, so pure, full of splendor and grace like an angel at my gravesite come to take me home. I haven't the words, but she did herself up special, clean and sparkly. She wore little or no makeup, her ivory skin radiant; her hair like a tropical waterfall, her breath like autumn, her words clearly spoken, above the line.

We took the train to the city. She talked Beckett. She was smart like an art historian, a politician on truth serum, held nothin' back. She didn't care what you thought, wasn't running for office. Beckett, what's little known by most had secretly aided the French resistance during the War. He was Joyce's apprentice, friend, confidant, but wouldn't marry his daughter. Beckett so loved Buster Keaton, she'd just finished a biography on Buster. He was a human rubber boy, his parents throwing him all around the stage, bending and contorting him into all shapes and sizes, banging him into walls, scrapin' 'im off floorboards. They toured with Houdini. In some cities they were accused of child abuse, even brought up on charges, but never convicted. Buster was the inspiration for some of Beckett's characters. They did make a film together late in their careers. *Waiting for Godot* was Jess's favorite play. I was off, off, off on a good foot; I could tell she liked me. Of course I was on my best behavior, no f-words until she said a few. She showed me her bracelets, emerald and onyx, silver and black gold. "Onyx is my favorite fuckin' stone, I love black." I already had us married with 3 kids, her making jewelry, me writing books. She'd be my guttural queen; I'd be the sewer king. (pause) The ashtray is full. Took my pills. Need another cup. Didn't answer the phone yesterday, wanted to talk to no one. I won't make the bed but strip the sheets. I need to run a few errands, but I don't know what I need. Pay the phone bill. Pick up a letter from my shrink for the courts. I'd overdosed, Jess called 911 and I got busted. It's ironic, call for help and go to jail. It happens. That feeling like you've died and gone to hell. Someone throws a cup of piss on you, and you lie there in your cell catatonic, can't move. The guard, he just laughs. 3 days without a shower or a phone call. (pause) Again the ashtray is starting over, this last cup. Straightened the cushions on the couch, the cigar cushion is backwards, on its black side in mourning. God, why is it me again who survives? Memory like bits, I'm so tired, pieces, dead soldiers, friends, lovers. (pause) I open a fresh pack of cigarettes. Why me? Why am I the lucky motherfucker? Where's my turn? Thumbing the stone until my heart goes blank. The rains have stopped, it's only gray anymore, no tears. I'm too old now, there's no bounce, bouncing back but for land mines. Keep seeing Rodney in the glass. Keep writing. It's too late, too early in the day for anything but this. I'm listening to the drip, dripping of the drainpipe, clicking my pen open and closed, blowing ashes from the page, writing it all down. I don't need another cup. (pause)

My disability has rendered me unemployable, a full-time scribe. I am the page. There are no dishes in the sink. This is the last train out. No whistles, church bells, or wind chimes. Just a page. My turn is coming. The production was mediocre but the play was brilliant. We held hands on the way to the train. It was a difficult thing but I forced myself, grabbed hold of her hand. God, I was so fucking clumsy about it, awkward, but she smiled, seemed pleased, and took gentle hold of my hand. Would I get a kiss goodnight?

The train was packed, a Friday night, we didn't get a seat. "Saturday crowd," she said.

"It's Friday,"

"Oh." (pause) The coffee pot's rinsed; I'm out of cough drops, got milk. Can't eat just yet. We were laughing at ad posters. There was one for hemorrhoid cream, this poor taxi driver who had to sit all day. "What a pain in the ass that must be." She was spontaneous, whatever came into her head, told the truth. On the other side was an ad for the planetarium depicting glowing rings circling Uranus. A suit standing alongside us looked up from his paper, and in all seriousness asked, "How many rings around Uranus?"

"None, I hope. How many rings around your anus?"

Me, I chimed in, "Might wanna try some Preparation-H." The guy was stunned. We got hysterical, teary-eyed. Jess almost wet herself.

"Oh, yes, I get it!" He chuckled, "Stepped in shit, didn't I?" We all laughed.

I'd known no real love, a few high school crushes, but nothing serious. Might Jess be the one? All the sex I'd had were whores, really just hungry, War-ravaged Vietnamese women looking for a meal. (pause) The War had left me hypervigilant. In part thanks to Myles, I possessed a keen sense of awareness, could smell danger far off, knew everything going on around me, every movement and sound. A constant state of alert. Had no choice, it was ingrained in my subconscious, any conflict, enemy encounter, somehow I knew it all before it happened. I could distinguish a rocket's whistle a mile away, amid outgoing artillery, all the noise of friendly fire, loud music, and the chatter of a poker game. Others caught off guard would follow my lead. Table, money, and cards would go flyin' as I led the charge to the floorboards. (pause) The light is orange now, the coffee pot rinsed. Here comes the rain again in buckets. (later) Clean sheets, but no nap. Ran all my errands, got a new black shirt without no buttons. All my best friends have jumped off the bridge, or hung themselves from barn rafters. Wiped a dead bug off the wall, the splatter from the pavement. That's me stuck to the sole of your shoe, between the cracks like lines of page. This is all I know how to do, all that matters, if it matters at all. Blackbird squawking, wants my flesh. A gust of wind frees me up. Another cup, another cigarette. Need some good news like Lazarus come back from the dead. Hasn't anybody read my book?

Got a rejection letter from the producer of *Jar Head,* he's taking a break from War stories. Obviously he's got his head in a jar, or hasn't he noticed? This administration ain't taken any fuckin' breaks! I could use some War relief. Can't watch the news; keep seeing my old friends in the faces of young boys dying over there. It's over, songs like *Over There.* "It's a grand old flag; it's a high flyin' flag." It's all over now. I can't wave no flag anymore. Myles always said, "We don't belong here, we can't win this fuckin' War!" Idiots! I'm embarrassed for you. Hasn't history taught you anything? You can't defeat an enemy if you don't know who the enemy is; besides, home is where the heart fights strongest. We were once insurgents, guerrilla fighters, patriots, unstoppable!

The bed's made. There ain't a dirty shirt in the house, but only one that ain't blood stained. The music stops. Can't seem to get excited about tonight's reading, but I need to rehearse. Need for this coffee to work. Need for something to work. (long pause) Made a few phone calls, but I'm the only one home. I do believe the words are there, I just need to read them. That was my last sip. These feelings are all that seem real anymore in a world made of glass. The ashtray is clear, my lungs are black. I'm only killing time, making killing worth my while. What's been too long already, waiting on eternity in a handbasket. Again to fill the page. Thumbing the stone. My middle finger extended between the lines of page at whoever is responsible for this shit! I'm above the line like *the last dead soldier left alive*. I've smoked more cigarettes than anyone I know, any man alive. Shot more dope than Billy Boy, but I never shot my wife.

*   *   *

Lost another day, wrapped inside a still small package. Missed my cancer doctor appointment, made two others the day before, two out of 3 ain't bad. Took my pills as prescribed, made up for lost sleep. Feel alive. The mess ain't so bad; it's mostly under my skin. Just to get off this page. Keep thinking I'll be home free, but the page never ends. And the wind chimes, you can never go home again. If! If only in a handbasket. And all the good soldiers died tryin' to be good. I like the sound of leaves in wind, and the page turns all of its own accord. Above the line I know enough to know I know nothing. Less is missing, no greater than the whole, hole I'm in, bullets, buttons, and apart from. I'm dumber than a stone like a crumpled page, blood for ink at the price of fleshy gooseflesh. It's a beautiful day, yeah, but I only want out. A simple song, a clear view to the bottom, out from the glass. The water's deep, wiggles and divides, I'm a stick in the mud, a new-found mind set. And the gold finch in a feeding frenzy smacks up against itself. All vanity is glass. There's no one I'm looking for, but most likely Myles is dead like all us good soldiers.

There were a group of kids on the train, 4 guys, two girls, about 16 years old. They were talkin' Spanish, don't speak Spanish, but I could sense their hostility. Two more stops and we'll be off this train. I knew who their leader was. If shit goes down you always take out the Big Man, and everyone else backs off. Alone I feared no one, nothing, preferred being alone, but with someone else, especially a woman I felt responsible for their safety. That was my last sip. Empty the ashtray, rinse the coffee pot. The bed, it's already made. (pause) All clear. There are no dishes in the sink. Waiting, waiting on a still small package.

One more stop. Jess got quiet for a moment, noticed my attention wasn't on her, what she'd been saying. "You all right?"

"Yeah, just thinkin'."

"About what?" (pause)

"Ah, how many rings around Uranus?"

"Forget about it, buster!" (pause) Soup, I'll have some soup. (pause) I hate waiting. Last call for birds. Soup's gone. The Bag Man should be here, soon, before the light goes blind, before the walls collide, and the blind go deaf, and the deaf dumb, no nothing but this ringing in my ear.

"This is our stop." As we were getting off the train one of the girls came up behind Jess grabbed her by the hair, pulling it back, around and over her head, dragging her by the hair across the train, and took a seat. The girl's face was blank, stone cold expressionless, and void of any and all emotion, disengaged from the pain she was inflicting. Jess had her hands up, held on tightly to the roots of her hair to keep it from being pulled out. Oddly enough she never said a word, not a sound. No one on the train said or did anything, as if the incident wasn't happening, didn't exist, as if being surfed over like a bad TV commercial. I got my hand in there, in all that hair, attempting to pry the girl's hand loose. "Let go of her hair!" I repeated myself, directing my words and attention at the Little Big Man standing beside her. I didn't want those doors closing; we had to get off at this stop. There was nothing to think about; I knew what had to be done. I'd grab onto the handrail above with both hands, fly two legs into the air, one foot to the girl's jaw, her head would snap back, smack against the wall, she'd let go. My left foot…

*   *   *

I've alive and not well, and living at my desk. I'm grateful for the page, to be above the line where the words might find me. Another mess and everything hurts. I'm pumping my legs, black ink, and coffee. Still, I am of service, a soldier boy, a good scribe.

I had to get us off this train, me and Jess out of here before them doors slammed shut, and we'd be forced to ride one more stop. "Let go of her hair!" Looked Little Big Man in the eye, a quiet, piercing stare. *I'm gonna fuck you up!* Without saying it, I said it. And my left foot would fly into his crotch, driving his balls up into his brain. I'd give 'im a fuckin' head butt, break his goddamn nose! I was ready to leap, can't let these doors close. (pause) Took my pills, diabetes, blood pressure, antidepressant, got hep c, only thing I ain't got is AIDS. Splashed some water on my face, I'm still orange like a pumpkin. Two butts in the ashtray and this one I'm smoking. A look in the glass: it's better than being yellow I guess, a tan without ever going to the beach. It was that jungle land, the pot I'd been smoking, in retrospect, surely it was sprayed. We didn't know nothin' back then, but for stayin' alive. I was yellow once, the whites of my eyes, back when I met Bill Burroughs. I have a photograph. The birds are just beginning. Called in sick for court, my public defender wanted my shrink's letter, Harold ran it over. Never again will I let anyone call 911. Yes, I'll have one more cup, another throat lozenge, please, fuel my cough with another cigarette. They're picking up the trash, *beep, beeping*, the truck is backing up. All my guns are in that dumpster, you've got nothin' on me! All my windows are open, freeing me up from the stench of last night's debacle. I don't think anyone really lives here. God, it's only me on this page.

"Let go of her hair!" Don't know if I pried the girls hand loose, or it might have been Little Big Man repeating after me, "Let go of her hair." Anyway, Jess got free, and we got off that train just as the doors were closing. Caught our breath, "You okay?" Jess, attempting to untangle her hair, just nodded her head. We saw a cop on the platform, told him what happened. A young man approached, he'd been on the train, spoke Spanish, understood all that had gone down. Wouldn't want this to happen to his mom or younger sisters. The kids had box cutters, talked about havin' some fun, staging a ruckus. Little Big Man had ordered the girl to grab Jess by the hair; if I got physical, the gang would join in. Guess we were lucky; other than Jess's head hurting a little, and my senses booted to full alert, we remained unscathed.

Jess got real talkative with the cop, explaining everything in minute detail, in sharp contrast to the total silence she professed during the incident. She just curled up like a weary prizefighter against the ropes and held onto her hair. I didn't think too much about it back then, and none of it would make any sense until 30 years later.

I had this empty feeling about me like surviving a rocket attack, knowing there'd be another. I could taste death. I felt dirty, Jess seemed unclean. I could smell sweat, a puked scent of cum like when I walked into my tent and found that poor girl that big fat Master Sergeant Loopahole had raped sobbing hysterically. I would have killed 'im if it weren't for Myles. No, I can't describe the feelings, but I didn't want to hold hands anymore. Just wanted to go home, crawl up under the sheets and sleep it off. No kiss goodnight, I don't want one, didn't wanna be kissing anyone. One more cup, please. (pause) There's that train whistle again off in the distance. The memory of, If! If only she were alive I'd do it all differently. (stop) This last cup like a warm embrace, a sweet kiss goodnight. I need to make the bed, give the patio a sweep. I'm almost out of cigarettes. Got ink. And the wind chimes 3 beats, lonely, alone, and If! If only. All is vanity but for black ink.

The cop was gonna radio ahead to the next station, "What car were they on?" He'd have them arrested. Me and Jess we didn't know, but the young man had been keenly attentive. "3rd car from the rear."

*   *   *

Chapter 2

come here / go away

I said to myself, "Come now, I will test you with pleasure. So enjoy yourself." And behold, it too was futility. Eccl. 2:1

＊　　　＊　　　＊

My old friend Nancy called; after a detailed search she thinks she's got a phone number for Myles. Names, places, dates, all the information seems to fit. After all these years, is this really Myles? Has he been found? What to say? How he was all I trusted, believed in, loved. All else the War had ravished, but for Myles my soul survived. (pause) Disconnected, no forwarding number. And all the good soldiers cry real tears.

Once upon a time Shay had it all, everything, but like Job it was all taken away, and she was stricken with lesions. Two homes, diamonds, fur coats, a Mercedes. Her husband went to prison for embezzling, she knew nothing of his thievery, hadn't a clue. They took away all her worldly possessions, then her legs, her smile, her memory. As If! As if she'd fallen from grace.

Even if I know exactly how she is, how she feels, what she's doing, still, I can make her laugh, even if she forgets the joke, forgets she ever laughed at all about anything. Still, I can free her up, if only for a moment, from the bottom to the top, above the line. (pause) No answer.

A week had passed; we hadn't spoken. Jess was working at the college pub, pouring drafts, slapping mugs, pitchers full of frothy beer down on a bar full of insolent preppies. A shitty band was playin' pop chart AM crap, pawning off bad as good drinking music. I sat at a corner table in the back, a crowded room made less crowded by pounding back beers in the good company of John, a sculptor I'd recently met, a minimalist like me who shared my disdain for crowds and penny loafers. We were getting plastered, shit-faced, fall down drunk. (pause) The bed is made, the patio swept free of grass cuttings. It's a gray day without the tears; inside I'm freezing, words falling from a black sky like shooting stars into a bucket full of icy ocean. Jill's gone and kicked it! Need to make an appointment at the ENT clinic, have my cancer looked for. Again to soil the ashtray. And my desk lamp rattles its metal stand with each word I write.

Jess had served me one too many beers, had a few herself, like me she didn't care any for the band. She was pissed, didn't wanna be behind the bar, "Gotta serve too many assholes, it's part of my work study." It's how she was paying for college. Her parents could have easily footed the bill, but as a matter of principle they felt she needed to work for an education. Think I'll take a walk into town, get me some breakfast. (later) Got a new vinyl flowered shower curtain, poppies, cheap, disposable, two months of soap scum and toss it. I'm feeling disposable. Got enough smokes to last through the weekend, a new bath and hand towel. No phone calls, but my little purple sleep aid came in the mail, a short story from my nephew Jonathan. Haven't had a decent sleep all week. Keri had her baby, Ashley Ann, Shay's middle name is Ann, she's a grandmother now. (pause) Read Jonathan's story, he's talented, a gifted young writer and he's only 14, has a bright future. Called 'im up, encouraged him, gave him a few ideas, some books he should read. "I'm proud of you." Again to make the bed, it all starts with making the bed, even if I haven't slept. Again the ashtray is starting over. This last cup. This cough is spilling me over, inside out. Turn off the music. I really hated the fucking band, went up to the bar for one last beer. "I'm out of here," said Jess, taking off her pub smock, "Wanna come over?"

"Sure." Said goodbye to John Slaughter, we'd meet again. Me and Jess walked slowly up the hill toward the dorms; she was a little tipsy and I could hardly walk. I don't remember much what happened. "And if you were Willie Moore, and I were Barbara Allen," heard it playin' on the stereo. It had only been a year for me, out of the jungle and into this country life. She had all these empty Jack Daniels bottles lined up on the windowsill, 6 of 'em. Again I'm waiting on a phone call, a still small package, get me out of myself. Still, it looks like rain, my throat parched like a sandbox. How many more pages? How many more bullet holes before I disappear, before there's nothing left? Yeah, "I'm goin' back to Harlan." We had sex, I passed out. During the night her ex-boyfriend walked in, "God, I forgot to lock the door," she was upset at herself. They yelled a few obscenities, each at the other, he left disgusted. "He's old news, hurt me once too often." This was a first for me, first time I'd spent the night with anyone, must have been drunk enough that it didn't matter. Besides, she wasn't the enemy, this ain't the War, ain't no enemy here. That was my last sip. Rinse and clear. (pause)

Ashley Ann was born today, and she's already made it onto the page. Maybe someday she'll read this, get to know her Grandmother, feel the grace. As a kid Shay would run down the street chasing ambulances like some boys chase fire trucks. Wanted to help, was born with a predisposition, a basic instinct to care for others. She had no queasiness about blood, didn't recoil from death like so many do. Once she came home all excited, she'd held hands with a dying woman, helped her pray. "She looked into my eyes Mom, said, 'You're God's angel come to take me home.'"

Sunday morning, hung over, give me a couple aspirin and let me leave. Jess wanted a paper, so I drove her to the smoke shop, I needed cigarettes anyway. Jess didn't smoke, but she smoked mine. When we got back to her place I said goodbye at the door. She wanted me to come in, have some coffee, read the paper. "I don't read papers, there's no good news but for the sports page, besides, it inks up my fingers." She practically slammed the door in my face. She turned away from a kiss goodbye, knew I'd already left, and wouldn't be compromised by any formality. Jess was no fool.

Maybe it'll rain; if I have some tea with honey and lemon will my throat feel any better? A siren screams off in the distance. If! If Shay were here and healthy she'd chase after it, I'd go with her. (pause) Tried calling, wanted to read her a few lines, again no answer. I've got two pills I need to take with food. (pause) Opened a can of soup. Again to suck up the mud like all the good soldiers. I'm loosing weight fast, look like I did when I came back from the War. Soup's on. (pause) I might just go ahead and disappear like chicken broth. Again I'm only waiting on a still small package like a dog for a milkbone. If! If only for a moment's sway, a reprieve from all this insanity, and sadness. Kill the memory, like Shay forgets everything.

*   *   *

The Bag Man didn't show last night. Here's that rain I was waiting on, holy water, a sacrificial cleansing. Metal pings, drainpipe tings like pangs to the heart. And the wind chimes, still, no end in sight. Nothing it seems will ease the memory, even the good times now make me sad. I'm all alone here, I can't wash it away. I've got the whole day to endure, wait, just waiting my turn. My feet are blistered and hurt. It's a hard walk anymore, ankle-deep in mud, stuck in my boots. (still) Rodney's dead, and I can't find Myles anywhere.

A few days later, and I was really missing Jess, wanted to see her again. I'd never quite met anyone like her. Yeah, I'd been tryin' to close the door, and she slammed it shut, wouldn't tolerate my bullshit. Surely, I must have her! (pause) Took my pills, another cup. No, there ain't nothin' for me to do in the rain but write, sunny days are much the same, but at least I can take a walk. It's a cool gray morning; there are no birds at this moment. My cigarette slips from my hand to the floor. The rain smells like dead frogs belly up on River Road. Pop, pop, pop, small arms fire, Dayl's been hit, "Jesus!" I'm only missing in action. And the world slowly burns. I'm bunker bound and there's nowhere I'd be going to. Don't really want to be awake. I'm waiting, waiting on the words to find me, pull me out from myself. Is there anything of mine that hasn't been taken? (pause) Rich fixed my computer, twice he fixed it, but it'll break again. A fresh pack of cigarettes, footsteps on the ceiling. It's raining harder now. I turn the page, what should be effortless but everything hurts. This coffee isn't working, my throat screams, and my heart pines. "And if you were Willie Moore." The truth is killing me, I don't like myself. I'm tired of playing Lazarus, God, just let me be dead in a handbasket for all that eternity brings, like Shay Full of Grace forgets everything.

I had to see her again. She was all I wanted, all that mattered anymore. At first she wouldn't hear of it, wouldn't let me in, but I kept knocking, wouldn't go away. I was as tenacious as she. What ensued was a long, pleasurable, wonderful courtship, days full of spontaneous laughter, heartfelt talks, excitement, and walks in the woods, "Underneath the silver maples, the balsams and the sky." Nights by the comfort of a warm fire, telling our stories. "And grew up by and by," I'll have one more cup. (pause) "We'd popped the heads off dandelions." (pause) No, I can't go back to Harlan.

Again I've filled the page with nothin', just how the words have found me. Might take a walk in the rain; make myself sick with the flu. Didn't get a shot, don't wanna be immune. You see, there's a heightened state of awareness when you're sick and dying akin to autumn's colors, a clear scent of being alive. I'm alert, my senses are keen, I know every sound and heartbeat. I'm glued to the page, and under fire. The wrens fly about from bushes to birdhouse gathering twigs. I have no race with death but to finish this book.

We sat on the hillside below the old mansion, now the admissions office, sprawled out on the grass looking down on a foot of water, a concrete pool like the Dead Sea full of leaves, sticks, rodents, dead everything in a soupy green puss. (pause) Blackbird squawking in the distance, getting closer, I feel like Van Gogh in a haystack. "Weeping and pining for love." Again the ashtray is starting over. What isn't up to me, how the world behaves, who kills and dies, and is born again. The truth is all I'm feeling. I was on that hillside, all of me, nothing behind, nothing that hadn't been. What future's here, won't compromise that. Three nights before, before this hillside had ever been imagined, I set fire to all my words, a stack of notebooks knee high, a ceremonial blaze. Vanity went up in white smoke vanished me into a black wind. My eyes burned clean. I wrote something new, *The 3rd Light*, 3 pages, 3 parts, one run-on sentence, cinematic prose. "Movie mind man moves about with an instant eye, click, pigeons fly south on the New Jersey Parkway like moon craters and jungle talk, Ann of 1,000 washes melts into a plaster cast of the Virgin Mary…" A golden calf, the holocaust, Richard Nixon, all Man's futility was on them 3 pages, 3 parts, one sentence. Sitting on that hillside I read it all, all of it to Jess, all that was left, all I'd written. (pause) Tried calling Shay again, still no answer. I thought the rain had stopped, but it hadn't. Red bird tweaking at my window.

(still morning) No nap, nothin' but junk in the mail. The rain's finally stopped, the sun just shot through. Need to hit the store; I'm almost out of pretzels. Need some air. Need a house cleaning. (pause) Made a few phone calls. Again I'm waiting, waiting on nothing, to go nowhere but numb. Jess liked what I read, wanted a copy. I put it back in its envelope, "You can have this one," handed it over, "There ain't any copies." I lit a cigarette like a proud father might have a cigar, lit one for Jess. (pause) Another cup. Need to toss what doesn't work, my old stereo, empty lighters, pens, all my broken shoelaces, this key chain. My discarded match had caught the envelope on fire, I quickly stomped it out with the palm of my hand. Removing its contents I found the pages badly singed, but not a word had been lost. It started to rain. We made our way back to the mansion, waited out the storm.

Walking the path back to the dorms we held hands, everything was alive, a subdued palette, but bold broad strokes upon a desolate sky. I was like a tree, leaves turning, she the pond at my side, glistening, fish jumping. It was all true, complete, whole, above the line. We went back to her place, didn't have sex, but made love for the first time. Life was full of wonder.

"Come here, and hold me." It was all I wanted, and did. "Don't leave." I never wanted to. (pause) The ashtray is full; my cup's all but empty. The music stops. I'm thumbing a cold smooth stone. When I'd be leaving she'd say, "When you comin' back, Red Ryder?" It was from a play she liked. I'd have to say, "Never!"

"Say it again."

"Never!"

Now she's the one who ain't never comin' back. God, I'm stuck like handprints in cement, just can't get my feet on the ground. No, I can't get back to Harlan. (later) In need of a phone call, somethin' to get me off this spot. Again to make the bed, but I can't move. Where are my angels? Is there no saving grace? There's an eagle at the end of my cigarette burning bright, burning me orange. I'm like a man without a country. Talked with my Vietnamese neighbor, Huong Ly, she's so grateful for her freedom, thanks me for being a soldier. I only want to cry. Huong puts both hands together over her heart, and bows. Talks of respect, respects me more than any American ever has, and knows how it feels not to be free. (pause) You can throw it all out with the trash, but you can't silence the words. No one calls; no one wants to hear it. I've no one to tell anymore, what's confined to the page. Yes, I've tasted the blood, can't rid myself of the smell. The price of freedom. (pause) One phone call, but not the one I wanted, I've nothin' to say. Just this page, and who's listening? You can't start what's already finished. It's tumultuous from here on out. Ain't no Harlan here! A train whistles off in the distance, where the sun and sky meet the tracks like a hangman's cord, "For the hangman's reel." God, I'm only failing.

*　　　*　　　*

Another morning after, lost a day to sleep. My left hand is swollen, full of pin pricks. Again to toss the trash, used guns and bloody shirt. I'm before the birds, before the sky. Above the line, out of view, but for reflections in the black glass. I'm a ghost. Had dreams where more than the bottom fell out, mud floors like sweltering pots of goop. There's no bouncing back but for land mines. I'd been cut in two again. Could do the morning meeting, nourish my better half. I've got a reading tonight with a group of veterans; I'll keep myself small at a back table. My feet are cold. Need to clean myself up, need cigarettes. Don't know where I'm going, just where I've been. Step, word, flesh. Spirit is all that isn't futile. Didn't answer the phone yesterday, didn't miss a thing. She's all that I'm missing. I've got metal in my mouth. Junked that old stereo, the speakers off the walls, that big box of a subwoofer. You could fit me in a duffel bag, a handbasket; ship me back home, out from this War. *Don't care much about nothin'* I thought, *only this page*. Need to take my pills, one more cup, fill 'er up. (pause) 3 butts in the ashtray. I'm lookin' through the glass. The trash is out, it's cold outside, took my pills. The garbage truck should be here soon, eradicating all you've got on me. Don't know about the meeting; don't trust myself not to strangle the Big Man. It's lonely here on the page, being a killer, waiting on the sky like a child crawls, yearns to walk. Can't get this metal taste off my breath. Need a view beyond the glass, my ghostly self.

I'm off that page, above the line where there are no health issues. No guns or white flake, no craving. Me and Shay were in the back seat, I was 7, and she was 6. Mom left the brake off, ran into the flower shop, Uncle Al's place. We started rolling down the hill, "Oh my goodness!" Shay screeched. I tried climbing over, into the front seat, I wanted to drive. Some stranger with big burly hands dropped his dry cleaning, jumped into our car and slammed on the brakes. We were saved! Still, I was disappointed; I'd missed an opportunity to get behind the wheel. Mom felt badly, offered to pay for his dry cleaning, "It ain't necessary, Ma'am" his clothes hadn't gotten dirty, they were wrapped in plastic.

Made that appointment with the ENT clinic. 10 months ago I had my surgery, they cut from just below my left ear to the center of my throat, removed a growth the size of a golf ball. That was just the spread of it, still haven't found the primary, the source, where it's coming from. They wanted me to do radiation, some chemo, put a stomach tube in for feeding because I wouldn't be able to swallow. Everyone wanted me to do it, Mom, my friends; it didn't matter to Shay. All she ever asks, "Are you being good? Where does this come from?" My brother John said he'd lend me some money if I took the treatment; I needed it to pay off the Bag Man. He wanted me to sign a waiver giving him permission to obtain information, talk to doctors, monitor my progress. I didn't like the stomach tube idea, having another surgery. Went back and forth, indecisive, said yes once just to please my mom, but eventually opted out, couldn't be bought. Rinse and clear. (pause) Think I'll do the meeting. *Beep, beep, beep*, the trash is being picked up. (later) It's cool enough that one wants to stand in the sun, feel its warmth, and be on that side of the street. My windows are open just a crack, *smoke exit*. Not much of a nap. Did the meeting, had breakfast with Romulus. Got some pills in the mail, that's it. Could do some laundry, but I'm not pressed for a clean shirt. Got Ms. Jones on the box, "Hey, Mister, can we have our ball back?" I'd like it that simple, a snowy morning, riding a milk crate, and the clanking of bottles. Catbird on the back lawn, "Purr, purrrrr." A giant yawn just like a tunnel mountain pass, light comes from rock. Cough, coughing, and the ceiling falls through, and again there's no mountain left standing.

A few months ago the Doc said I'd already passed the point where I would have benefited from the treatment, "Sometimes the patient knows best." No, they haven't found it; don't even know if I've still got cancer. It hasn't come back, but I believe it will. Don't know what to believe, but eventually you gotta take a bullet. (pause) Start it up again, the page, the music, and the ashtray. Give me back Jess! Do I make the bed, or wash the sheets? Think I'll have sushi for lunch. Sometimes I feel invincible like where the word meets the page. Sometimes I wish it would stop. (again) My windows are dirty, this is a pig's pen, and I'm makin' heavenly mud pies. Get me out of range; all of it triggers this old War news. More pills in the mail, a whole box full. Had my lunch, now I'm sinking. Only want to be a perfect yawn, a moment void of time where nothing's the same. Right here, now, everything hurts. Was Lazarus grateful, or pissed? This last song has no words. I'd like to crawl up into soft feet, an infant's PJs. Saw a red bellied woodpecker today and a rabbit behind the bus shelter being devoured by a hawk. I'm a small, too short to be plucked, stout, proud weed in your organic vegetable garden. I've come back from Harlan, and I'm here to remind you. (pause) Shay full of grace doesn't know enough to kill herself, forgets she wants to.

*   *   *

Lost another day. It's a gray morning. No sign of life. 4 phone messages. My left hand like a pink balloon, can't make a fist. Again the computer's down. This cup is golden, like silk on my sandpaper throat. Need a new computer. Talked to Larry, my writer friend, therapist, maybe he can get me some help. (pause) Another cup. Jess made the best coffee. Need a few things from the store, I'm out of pretzels. Need to air out the place, rid myself of this blood smell. Morning fog over the back wood like a lost dreamscape. Blue jay squawking like a prisoner set free. The cats upstairs are running track, little feet, pitter, patter, back and forth. I'm waiting for the fog to lift. Don't know where I'm going with this story, what to say, or even if I want to say it.

Don't know which cat won the race. What difference will it make if the fog lifts? Again the ashtray is starting over. (pause) I've got mine fields up my sleeve. Again I've filled the page with nothing. Come here and go away, it's the language of love. I was washing dishes and a soapy bowl slipped from my hand to the floor and broke. It was a bowl her brother made. Jess got furious, started screaming at me, crying, hurling obscenities and silverware. "It was an accident." She didn't want to hear it.

"You clumsy fucking asshole!"

"Picasso, we're not related." I couldn't make her laugh, defuse her anger. She hit me in the chest with a fork. There was nothing left for me to do; I took my things and left.

I wonder if Shay knows, remembers she's a grandmother. Can she hold Ashley Ann and smile, feel the grace? (pause) Only junk in the mail. Two letters, the kind you rip up and throw out and don't even have to open. Don't need car insurance when you don't own a car. (pause) My clothes are in the wash, the laundry room's 3 doors down, $1.50 a load. Ain't so bad, I can write while I wait. 'Tis the season to flip my mattress, wash a few windows. (pause) Called home, home has always been where my parents live, left a message. They've been married 60 years plus, and I've never been in a relationship that lasted longer than a year. They're each others best friend. Atlantic City's their favorite getaway. Mom plays the nickel slot machines, Dad blackjack. Mom always said Jess would leave me in the end, "She wants to settle down, have children, and you're so aloof, noncommittal." She was right. After me Jess married the next guy she dated, the kid came much later. (pause)

My clothes are in the dryer. Larry called, he might be able to help me, get me into treatment where he works. I need something other than the VA, they only keep me stuck, want me dead, so they don't have to pay. (pause) Clean sheets, thought I lost a sock, but I found it. The light streaks through the blinds, falls across my chest like a prison suit. Did the store, the pretzel bin is full. Got some fruit, soup, cheese, toiletries. It's all vanity.

When I was diagnosed with cancer all the doors flew open, all the help, concern, compassion I needed, but if you say PTSD (post traumatic stress disorder), mental illness, or addiction the doors slam shut. If I were missing a limb, yeah, they could understand that. There's a social prejudice that exists across the board, as If! As if it were my fault. "You volunteered for Vietnam," my mother once told me. My only response: "Does a fireman volunteer to get burned?" A rape victim gets treated like a rapist: "If you didn't dress the way you did. If you didn't jog in the park after dark." As if we didn't have enough ifs in our heads, enough guilt that I can't bury the dead. (pause) Another cup. I need another still small package before I take a shot at redemption. It's a beautiful day, but I don't feel so beautiful. My stomach hurts as if lemon and milk were curdling up inside me. It's all slow going, broken treaties, and no place like home. The music stops. (pause) Again to make the bed, and I didn't even get a nap. Made a few phone calls, everyone's busy but me. Talked to Keri, Shay held the baby and smiled, "There's a picture you should see!" All Shay can do these days is slowly feed herself; if you pick her up her legs just hang there like meat on a rack, limp like a puppet without any strings. Can't remember short term, nothin', can't hold a conversation. She only shits her diaper anymore. Yes, Shay Full of Grace smiled again while holding her granddaughter, Ashley Ann! And the wind chimes gloriously.

All the mirrors are made of glass, flat and predictable. Don't know where or how this chapter ends. Jess took fewer drugs than me, but like me she was a drunk; she'd accuse me of corrupting her, worsening her bad habits. Over the years we've both had long periods of abstinence; still, I'm real upset she's gone and left without me. 3 weeks before she died we'd gone to a meeting, she hadn't been drinking, life was good, her business flourishing, she seemed happy. Jess and Maria left that evening for the Island. Spent 3 weeks at her parent's vacation home. Barbara said, "I believe she started drinking again after about a week on the Island. Called me drunk off her feet one night, slurring her words, couldn't make any sense of what she was going on about." Why? If! If she'd only called me. I would have, could have, but, but what isn't up to me. She'd been sober almost a year. What happened? She'd only been home a few days when Harold found her dead. Church bells. This rusty cough rings a few bells in my head. (pause) A 6 o'clock church recording plays *Ode to Joy* out across the Village airways.

I was living in the dorms temporarily, rehearsing a play. One night Jess came over late, drunk, mad as hell. We were on the skids, I'd been distant, was bailing out. She was fuckin' nuts like what love does when scorned. I'll empty the ashtray, rinse the coffee pot. (pause) Why am I playing this music? It only makes me miss her more, remember all my mistakes. *Crazy love.* I told her she had to leave. Jess threw herself on the living room floor and started kicking with them construction boots like a child throwing a tantrum; she woke up my downstairs neighbors. "Shit!" I could hear Big Charlie comin' up the stairs, didn't know what to do. I placed my foot on her stomach, applied a little pressure in hopes of stopping her kicking. There was a knock at the door. "Open the door!" Charlie stood there half asleep, pissed; we'd woken him and Emma up. Jess left screaming, "He kicked me, he fuckin' kicked me!" Of course Big Charlie thought that was what all the kicking was about. I tried telling him what had happened, but he'd already been convinced by them big watery green eyes, "He kicked me," like an owl shrills the night awake, "He fuckin' kicked me!" And Big Charlie believed her. Before I'd finished my explanation he'd landed a hard right to my face, put me flat on my back, my nose and lip gushing blood, out cold. Broke my fuckin' nose! "You don't hit a woman!" He guffawed, "Asshole!" I didn't hear him say it, but the whole dorm did.

One summer I visited Jess at her parent's vacation home. We made love in the woods by the creek, back behind the stadium. It's that part of the song that always gets to me, that and sitting by the fire listening to *Into the Mystic,* "We were born before the wind." Other than that I didn't care much for Van Morrison back then. Was grateful Jess didn't have brown eyes, even if she sometimes pretended to be that girl. Need to take a walk. Killed a tiny spider, so tiny it could fit itself on the head of a pin. It moved across my desk, attached to my notebook by a thin thread; I'd move my notebook, and it would move with it. I crushed it with my thumb. (pause) Maybe it was a tick. The bed's made. Can't believe this War-riddled soul of mine just might be writing a love story. Don't you believe it. Who would have thought, not me, not Jess, but it's the story that's writing me. It's the truth. Should floss my 6 remaining teeth.

Jess thought it cruel and unusual punishment that I'd make her listen to Jethro Tull. "Tull rhymes with dull, you're an asshole." I hated when she called me asshole, that Picasso retort saved me from rage, kept the veins in my neck from popping out. It was the same thing with my mother, she'd nag, nag, nag, relentless. I'd learned something from my younger brother Billy, he'd call my mother by her first name, Nat, her name's Natalie, "Okay Nat, yeah Nat, I'll do it your way, Nat." She'd laugh and lose track of what she was nagging about. This was a valuable lesson; it stopped me from throwing things, punching walls, breaking glass. Jess didn't always laugh, but she'd usually give up the attack. Think I'd heard my mom call my dad asshole too many times while he was still drinking. Didn't wanna be Son of Asshole. Blue jay squawking. (pause) Had my soup, right out of the can, from the pot, no bowl, complete with vegetables, just like being in the bush. I own only one spoon, one butter knife, one fork, one bowl, but I only use it for cereal. My spoon's multipurpose. Had a salad for lunch. I'm thumbing a stone. I'd like to watch the news but it only upsets me, can't watch no Wars, still, can't live like an ostrich. And what have you learned? Nothin!

Bought a good book today, but I won't tell you what it is, I'll read it first. (pause) The Bag Man called. I'm only waiting now on another still small package. I'm gonna really try not to kill myself tonight. What I need is some heavenly aid, keep myself alive, between the lines, scribble, squawk, these black marks like cave drawings. I love blue birds.

*   *   *

Lost another day, the ringer off. No phone messages. I always feel more alive the day after, the clarity of having survived. My hand is fat and pink. Can't take much more of this dancing with the enemy, stomping through the jungle, being shot at. I'm up before the sky, before the birds, me and the crickets waiting on a train whistle. Unfortunately that's me in the glass wearing a long face. Our relationship lasted about a year, the last few months it was back and forth, come here and go away. Over and again, no one it seemed could make the split. Still in love, but full of indecision, anger, animosity, hurt. The past was greater than the day. Jess became like the War, a land mine, an enemy attack. Think I reminded her of her dad, but hadn't a clue what that was about. (pause) Another cup. Need some water on my face. Need to be any color but orange. Of course the VA attributes my cancer to smoking, but 3 out of 5 people in my group, all with the same type of cancer, never smoked. The VA as a matter of practice repeatedly denies everything, any responsibility, doesn't want to pay. Took 'em 25 years to finally admit I'd been traumatized, had PTSD, wanted to blame everything else but the War. My childhood, mental health, my father's drinking, my drug-taking, after I'd been clean almost 9 years that excuse no longer applied. (pause) Made that appointment with the ENT clinic. Am I repeating myself? The ashtray is full. *Ring, ringggg…* I don't answer it. I need something like a walk on water, like skipping stones across a frozen lake. *Ringgg…* a band of matter circling a planet, dust particles, small bodies. *Ringgg…* rings on her fingers, and toes. *Ringgg…* bands that circle Saturn, Jupiter, Uranus, and Neptune. (pause)

Again the ashtray is starting over. It was Barbara left a message, an old college, jeweler friend of Jess's. Should eat something. Don't think she ever liked me much. Guess she's hurting too, missing Jess, feeling the loss of a good friend. No, I'd never give it up, but this stone would skip great. Need Harold and his milk truck. A never-ending train whistle. I need Jess in my life, alive again. God, get us all aboard the last train out.

She finally shut me out, changed the locks, "Get the fuck away from me, I never want to see or speak to you again!"

"Really?"

"Really!"

Again it was my fault, like with Rodney; it was me who wandered off into that mine field. "Short! 3 days, and a wake up," he howled like a lone wolf atop the highest mountain, "I's one lucky motherfucker!" And Rodney should have, If! Made it back to the World. I'll have one more cup, but can't stop the thoughts. (pause) It was now I wanted her more than ever, once she'd slammed the door shut forever. Wanted her more than life itself, like all of what I can't have. I felt so helpless, nothin', but nothin'

to be done about it like a rocket attack, you just gotta lie there, suck up
the mud! "Jesus fuckers!" Can't bring Rodney back. Jess had moved out of
the dorms, rented a house, alarmed all the windows and doors. She'd look
through the peephole, and if she saw it was me she'd latch the deadbolt
shut. "Go away!"

"Get off my fucking phone!" More than once she slammed the phone
down on my ear.

Above the line there are no phone conversations, no knock-knock
jokes. I don't have to take my pills, no one has to die. No air, no inhaler,
no deadbolts. (pause) Jess pressed charges, repeated phone calls for the
purpose of annoyance. They took my photograph, fingerprints. "No, that
wasn't my purpose, annoyance, no sir! How do I get this ink off my hands?"
The last time I saw Jess was in a courtroom, and not again until 30 years
later. She dropped the charges, but only after the judge made me promise
I'd never call or go see her again.

She was upset, nervous, kept stumbling over her words, repeating herself.
Our friends sided with me, were there in the courtroom intimidating her,
hard cold stares, forcing her hand. You could hear a silent plea like static
over the airways, *drop the charges, bitch!* Her only advocate, friend in the
court room was Barbara. In summation the judge asked Jess if she was
okay with the arrangement. Her voice crackled, "Only if he promises never
to contact me again!" People laughed.

"We've already established that Miss."

I felt sorry for her, she was a mess. Sorry for me, I only wanted to cry.
I would never be her Willy Moore, or she my Barbara Allen. God, just let
me die. (pause) There's that train whistle again, the distant memory of a
life, a life gone by.

*   *   *

Chapter 3

30 years later

So I hated life, for the work which had been done under the
sun was grievous to me, because everything is futility and
striving after wind. Eccl. 2:17

＊   ＊   ＊

The sun is up. I'm all cleaned up, look good on the outside. I'll do the
meeting, just, just because, even if I'll get loaded tonight. (pause) Walked
to the meeting, under the sparrow tree. Bird shit on the pavement looked
like wedding rice, church bells were playin'. Black-capped chickadees
circled my head like a starry night, like words on a page, wind in my face.
The Crazy Man who lives across from the church sat on his butt curbside,
mumbling, rocking back and forth, pulling weeds from the grass where
there were none. Didn't take his medication, I guess it's more fun that way,
as if the wind had graced his life with genius. (later) A good nap. In my
dream I held Jess in my arms crying, apologizing. There was this thin film
between us so that we couldn't quite touch, like seconds, ceilometers, the
gap between life and death like the fine line between cretin and genius.
Soon, soon enough I won't have to make the bed anymore, there'll be no
coffee pot to rinse. I will be like a tree, like the word. I will be invisible

like the wind. Above the line nothing is still, and no one is moving. If! If you think you're doing it, you're not. There's nothing to talk about. (pause) Talked to Barbara, she's missing Jess too. She also has a key chain Jess made, but not a thumbing stone. Again I'm waiting on a phone call, again to make the bed. This last cup. Again I need out, out from this cloud cover, out from this flesh. I'm addicted to the edge, tossing swine from the cliff, the Mad Man and all his chains.

I heard she got married, moved to Vermont, was making jewelry and writing greeting cards for Hallmark. I moved to the city, found CBGB's, shot heroin, and wrote a few poems. "I love you more than love can be no less than any fool, whose dreams spring no more, and days do wait the night. Once here, twice removed and later. Others won't relate the pleasure of a smile, and only laugh a casual goodbye." She was having a country life, had married Big Charlie, I was in grad school, chasin' a bag, lost film footage. One butt in the ashtray and this one I'm smoking. I'm listening to Bob, when you listen to Bob there ain't nothin' else you can do. He demands all your attention. I miss Rodney, Myles, and all the rest of me I could have been. We're all good soldiers. Eat something. (pause) And all we eat is mud from cans. I'd walk windy city streets, tall buildings in my hair. They won't get us here tonight will they Mr. Dylan?

*   *   *

Black glass. It's me there, a day later, years past. One giant mess. Cats scampering above. I'm almost out of everything, need milk, no pretzels. Got cigarettes, coffee, a few cans of soup. Now it's my right hand that won't close. Spilled a bin full of pretzel crumbs between the counter and the fridge, scooped 'em up, fed 'em to the birds. Even if there are no birds yet. It's a Sunday morning; this coffee's working, two days from my ENT appointment. It must have rained; I can hear the metal pings of the drainpipe like time ticking out. All my life's insanity, relationships, jobs, all for nothing. Above the line there are no silver, no bronze stars, no victories, and no War heroes. All the dead soldiers are good soldiers. How I came to write my last book doesn't seem important, it was a happy accident. Like shit happens, so does grace. Still, I'm trying to keep my name off that outer wall. Still, part of me doesn't care in the least. Again to make the bed, fill the page, take my pills, and endure this day, this life. Nothin' but bullet holes, mine fields and fleshy bits like Mother Goose has run amok. I lit my coffee cup and drank my cigarette. The ashtray is full. I'm only waiting my turn. (pause) Again to clean up this mess, put out the trash, toss them guns out for good. That pen just ran out of ink. Again I'm starting over, but it's a lie, what I am is almost finished. Soon there will be light, a view upon the back wood, birds will gather at my loveseat, eat my pretzel crumbs. And a lone mourning dove will coo and pine away. Please erase my face from the glass. There are no tall sail ships coming into port, no exotic spices from the Orient. Dear Jess, I've no ribbon for your hair.

A few months after my book came out I got a card in the mail from Jess, first I'd heard from her in 30 years. On the cover was a pant leg of a woman, hands on a broom sweeping up a pile of dead leaves.

I hope this note finds you, I just read The Last Dead Soldier Left Alive *and felt compelled to try and contact you. Yeah…30 years.*

You are an incredible writer, the rhythm, your breath; your heartbeat is in every line.

I want to tell you how much reading your book meant to me, helping me understand what I couldn't 30 years ago. Thank you, Jess

If you are willing I would like to talk with you.

She left a phone number. Actually I didn't know how long it had been. The card came from Santa Cruz, California. 30 years, wow! My past came rushing up before my eyes, my legs started pumping, my pen began to sweat, my whole body swayed back and forth like riding on a freight train. This wasn't a joke like what God and the devil played on Job. I'd nothing left to be taken away. No, this was for real. What would I do?

I had no animosity, resentments toward her. It was a nice letter she wrote. I had no feelings either way, good or bad about her. Some 20 years ago I'd made amends, called her mom, knew better than to contact Jess directly. Asked Mildred to please tell Jess I was truly sorry for all the hurt and pain I'd caused her. Mildred thought Jess would be happy to hear it, never did hear anything back from Jess. Didn't expect any response. (pause) Had to splash some water on my face, open a few windows. That was Jess's picture window I'd written about in the last book, scribbled across with an Ivory soap sample, *I am the last dead soldier left alive.* Still, I'd moved on; let the past rest in peace. I had cancer, smoked too many cigarettes, and wasn't looking for a shot at redemption. There was no love in me left needing. Still, I was intrigued; I'd give her a call. Curious as to how the years had treated her. What was she doing? How had she changed? If she'd changed at all. 30 fuckin' years! What will be the same? Will there be anything about her I'll recognize? What page are we on?

Again I'll clean up this mess, make the bed. I'd call this minute if she weren't already dead. If! If it would make any difference. And the page turns. Blackbirds squawking in the distance over some dead thing, even roadkill has its purpose. I'm hungry. I can smell it, taste the blood like I'm baggin' Rodney all over again. Again, a large, almost-empty bottle of

Listerine on the coffee table. Why? Why is it always somebody else who fuckin' dies? All I've loved has been taken from me. All I can do anymore is scribble about it. All is grievous to me, all that's been done under the sun. Still, I'm striving after wind like some do for eternity in a handbasket. There's that train whistle again, vacant, flat, futile, the last train out.

*   *   *

Can't take much more of this being swollen and pink. Can't make a fist, couldn't throw a hard right if my life depended on it. Need to give up the fight game. Got the rest of the crumbs out from behind the fridge, fed 'em to the birds. I've got milk money. (pause) Left Robby a message, see if I can borrow his van, need a few things from the store, not much, just enough for a few days. Seems I've got no direction here, but Larry should come through soon, get me into his place, some heavenly aid. That pretty blue house of a postcard she sent me like my blue block of wood, one, one branch of blue sky, but for these words, and you can never go home again. (still morning) Got milk, bread, pretzels, sugar-free ice cream, cheese, cereal. Need a nap. (later) Some sleep but not enough; it's never enough, always wanting more. Can't live off that last page, seems there's always another page to fill. Music playin'. It's a beautiful day, beautiful enough but the past seems greater than who I am. It's too much. Can't fit myself out from these bullet holes, tight, tighter yet, I'm falling off the highwire and into a knot. All knotted up, missed the net, off the charts, can't stop the thoughts. It was me who wandered off in a bad direction. Just why Rodney isn't here anymore. (pause) The mud is deeper than my boots, can't find my fuckin' bootstraps. It's filling my throat, choking me to death.

We talked for two hours, all I recognized was her laugh, even her voice had changed. Still, we can make each other laugh. Everything else about her was different somehow like a distant train whistle grows further away with each passing year. *And we grew up by and by.* 30 years worth, 30 years from here. She'd gotten divorced from Big Charlie a few years back, has a 13-year-old daughter, Maria, Maria Full of Grace, she's the light in Jess's eye, everything she lives for. Jess is making jewelry, has her own business, works from home, no more greeting cards for Hallmark. She's made bracelets for Tina Turner, earrings for Annie Lenox, has a strong celebrity clientele; she's much in demand, more than enough work. Seems there's a line outside her door, a waiting list. *Why are you talking to me?* Didn't say it but wanted to. She felt she understood me now, now that she'd read my book. Now she knew why I behaved the way I did back then. I didn't understand me, my past, but maybe she did know me better than I do.

She defiantly understood what she was all about, knew more about herself than I know about anything.

*   *   *

I can use Robby's van and get me to the cancer doctor. 9 phone messages yesterday, I'd left the ringer off. Again I spilled the pretzel bin last night while eating pretzels in the dark. Got the shits. That's one of my favorite things to do, eat pretzels in the dark with my teeth out. I love the salt; make 'em soft and soggy, gum 'em to death. My arms are in bad shape, both hands pink and swollen. Never used to go below the wrist, but I've crossed that line. (pause) A couple more days and I'll be off to Larry's place. It looks nice outside; don't feel half bad considering I haven't slept. I'll toss the trash, make the bed, clean myself up. Again to rid the bathroom of that blood smell. Above the line we are all forever, Jesus isn't crucified again and again. There's no suffering, no pain, only good works. Like he said, "Only God is good." I am but a scribe, a blue line on a blank page. Life is futile, contradictory. I guess, imagine Jesus felt good while healing the sick like I feel when the words do find me here. This is my job, my place, my gift; if not for this I would surely perish. Yeah, I do believe in us our father is well pleased. Another siren, and the whole world is screaming in the distance, the sun burns too hot, eternities ablaze. God, it's just a page. 3 butts in the ashtray, and an empty black cup. If! If only for giving, won't you give me a read?

Jess is coming east to visit her family, is gonna stop and see me. I don't know what to think, how to act. What to believe anymore. If she'd only actually come again. If! If Jesus might be resurrected one last time, come down from that cross. I'm like Lazarus bound in linen and sackcloth, sleeping in the tomb of the living, waiting on the word of God. Again I've filled the page with nothin'. (later) Had a cancer-free check up, two biopsies pending, still waiting on a silver bullet. I've no excuse now for leaving. Just get up and live! I'd give it all up, all of me, to have her walk in late in total disarray, dropping books, into that classroom again like the first time on angel wings like chariots afire, jeweled and crossing over, halos round her boot heels.

It's hot, too hot, more like summer than fall. Too hot to take a walk. Need to cut my toenails before I rip my socks. I'm tired of these pin pricks. Empty the ashtray. I'm looking in the glass, is it me or is it simply a smudge? I've been smudged over. The leaves are turning colors, slowly; slowly Shay Full of Grace can feed herself. I'm waiting on one more phone call, one last still small package. I don't belong here! They put a camera down my throat, but couldn't find the real me. "Puff out your cheeks." No, they didn't find me there. "Breathe through your nose." Not the real me. "Say eeee!" No, not me anymore. When I came home the front lawn had been dug up, mined, the ivy sprayed, bushes gone, our perimeter, a white picket fence was now black, Jesus nailed to the gate, claymores and trip flares like a crown of thorns, gun ships hovered above. When I got back here God was dead, there wasn't anybody home. Barbara Allen, married Jody, was Barbed Wire, and I wasn't Willie Moore anymore. So I bunkered up behind a wall of sand, oil drums like urns full of ashes, rocks, and bone chips. And nothin' got in, nothin' got out. There was nothin' I'd lose anymore. Grew my hair and beard 3 years long, until I met Jess. And again, when Jess died the whole fucking War came crashing back again!

*   *   *

A day later. Waiting on Larry. Need to turn this thing around. Need to get out from behind this rock. Stop, before it stops me. Suck up some wind. I can hear one bird chirping, a solitary last prayer. Tired of the blood, the mess, vanity in search of a vein. Need to do some laundry. God, help me, please. Stop me from sticking myself up; robbing myself of gifts. Again we fall below the line. I'll have one more cup. (pause) If Jess were here she'd help me, I do miss her so, but she's at the bottom of my bottom too, at the bottom of the page.

Above the line there's nothing to grieve, no one loses anything, and everyone comes to visit. I need to take my pills like a good soldier. I need to be of service. The ashtray is overflowing. I'm waiting on the words to find me. All that's reflected in the glass is my lamp light; the light of day has made me invisible. (pause) I'm airing myself out; all my windows are open now in search of breathing space. Step, word, I am but a scribe, flesh and blood. The ashtray is clear. I need to wash the sheets. Feels like I've been hit by that train. (pause) Heard the whistle, felt the memory but didn't heed the warning. It's a gray morning. Took my pills. My hair's unruly like a blue jay squawking. My wrists are pink and swollen. No more bloodletting, please. So Jess was coming to visit, coming here, I wouldn't push her away this time. Told her I couldn't be her lover, I'm too sickly, but could be a good friend. We agreed on that. (pause)

All my dirty clothes are in the wash. It looks like rain but no one's fooled. Summer should be over, but it's still too damn hot. My lamp light still burns in the glass. Don't know if this chapter's finished, where it ends, what to say next. I'm missing days, years, time from my story. Yeah, why even number the pages, there's no past, future, sequence of events. It's all sprayed throughout my head, flashback, forward, circlin' my brain, squarely on the chin. I should eat something, ground myself, try and take my place in the moment, among the living. This body only hurts, aches, my visions blurred anymore. I've wandered off in so many bad directions, I've survived too long. Which War is this? I will try again to put my house in order, be right-sized, one rock, one smooth stone skipping across the lake. This page is all I am. There's nothing I can tell you, you don't already know. Nothing so painful you haven't felt, no beauty yet to be revealed. Yeah, I might make you look at somethings you'd rather avoid, but it's your choice to do something about.

These last few sips. Again to put out the trash. I still don't believe she's dead, and what lives inside me still. I've got a pretty new flower on the kitchen table, but all I can smell is the blood. (pause) Swept the patio, put my clothes in the dryer. It's been a hard time of it since she's died like I'm missing a limb, my person abbreviated, can't complete a sentence. The workings of a red-bellied woodpecker, tap, tapping to the sounds of my own scratchings as I move across the page. A car drives by unseen like a rush of wind. Oh, to be silent. Soon the back wood will be naked, a pile of sticks like blue lines on a blank page. I will rise up above the grief in beauty and splendor like autumn's dying colors; take my last breath of wind. I will not await winter's sun, or a blanket of white to clothe my nakedness. Empty is free like this cup. God, it's only me here, poor of spirit. (pause) I believe this chapter's finished, but If! If this were eternity in a handbasket I'd leave you one, one branch of blue sky.

*   *   *

Chapter 4

words fall below

Therefore I completely despaired of all the fruit of my labor
for which I had labored under the sun. Eccl. 2:20

           *   *   *

The sun came out but I didn't like it. Made the bed, took a sleeping pill
and crawled back into it. No real mail, just an ad for a car I can't afford.
No dreams I remember. Need to clean myself up. (pause) Called Larry's
place, I'm goin' in tomorrow. Just to get past the urge, out from under the
thumb of it. I'm not so hopeful as if I'd had a dream. It's a hot, muggy
afternoon, I can't hear myself think. Everything's melting under the sun.
Words fall below the line. I'm not even half free, and the War don't ever
stop. Jess ain't comin' back! Death's like that, but for Jesus, Lazarus, and
me. Again, I'll have to do it again like another rocket attack, one more fire
fight. No, I never volunteered to get burned, champion the dead or enslave
the living. (pause) The days are too long. I've been too long under the sun;
I'm only wrinkled and swollen. Can't off my tiredness, that sleeping pill
effect, or is it the boredom, out from the killing fields, the fruitlessness of
my labor as the sun burns hotter than it's ever been. It's a sick, piss yellow
sun, hypnotizin' chickens; these eggs are bigger, better and golden! And

you believe it. God, I hate being awake. (pause) Just to get off this page, but it makes no difference. Another page will follow me, words falling down page after page. I feel so useless; I can't work miracles, heal the lame, make the blind to see, raise the dead, bring water forth from rock, into wine, or float bread from the sky. I'm not so busy dying or being born. I'm just here on this page out of necessity. (pause) I called Shay, but no answer. There's nothing I could tell her she'd remember anyway. Just wanted to say how much I love her, but she knows that. And I know I could have made her laugh. (pause) One last cup and one last cup to wash. The only mess you don't have to clean up is your dying mess, but you'd best leave your house in order. I've been so many pages on this desert, and in the distance the heat rises off the pavement like an oasis is sure to happen. But it's just where the sky meets the tracks like a hangman's cord, like an oil slick burning bright, and the music stops.

3 butts in the ashtray and wise men come, friends of Job, they make me laugh. And the wind chimes for the first time in days, there's even a breeze. (pause) I made all the phone calls I need to make, and only one person was home, but sleeping. Am I only looking forward to the past, Jess's visit, the best of times? Tall sail ships coming into port, she waves from the dock, my face at sea, a salty pose, wings on the heels of my boots. Like Lot's wife I've got it all backwards, this ship is leaving. *Row, row, row your boat*, my hands are rowed to the bone for table scraps. Still, I have no complaint; like a good scribe my words fall at my master's feet.

There are no living seafarers any longer, and all the dead poets have been molested. When Jess came to visit she told me all her secrets, things I'd never expected. I'd been shocked, more than surprised to learn she'd been sexually abused by her father. He wasn't that sweet, kind, gentle, caring family man, the loving dad I thought he was. God, I only hated him anymore, the more I heard my vengeance flared, a wrath that wanted him tortured, and killed! How could he? From the age of 9, he'd fuel her full of drinks and have his way with her, into her twenties until she got married. Night after night he'd be there in the shadows at the foot of her bed, or she'd dream herself awake, hands groping her warm places in the dark. Fuckin' Jack! "I have difficulty telling anyone, I was an adult and couldn't stop 'im, others, they act like I enjoyed it!" I handed her a fresh box of blue Kleenex, put my arm around her.

"It's how they treated me when I came back from the War."

"I wouldn't come home sick from school, they'd call 'im, I was afraid, I was always afraid he'd leave work and come home."

"It ain't your fault."

Words fall below like the gut-wrenching truth. If! If you ain't uncomfortable yet you'll never understand. How does one live with this, being raped, cast out, then stoned to death? I tell you, no one survives! She was 14 when Mildred and her brothers found out, but like her family she pretended it never happened, and if it did it wasn't happening anymore.

Now did Jess, she hasn't gotten here yet, actually tell me all that, or was it just a bad dream?

*   *   *

Friday morning, 6:35, September 28, no, I haven't slept. I'm leaving in a couple hours for Larry's place. They're picking up the trash, or is it thunder? I'll throw some shit in a bag. Ah, where are the words? I don't feel like I'm dying right now, don't need another minute. Should I pray? For what? Who for? "God bless Tiny Tim, Mr. Scrooge, oh, and help lower these hairs on the back of my neck." What I need is one of them overnight spiritual conversions. Blackbird, squawk, squawking, do I dare stomp my feet?

It's me in the glass waving goodbye, waving back at me. I don't care about the blood. I'm not really here. It's a snowy day; I'm ridin' shotgun on Harold's milk truck. We're stopped at a train crossin', them rails flashin', speed lights pulsing through my veins, all yellow, and orange and Xmas red like I'm Red Ryder, and I ain't never comin' back! I don't care about the milk! Who cares about the story? That she's dead! Don't care about fuckin' Rodney! I don't care if I never see Myles again! (pause) Words fall below. Yeah, it was me wandered off. The guardrails lift, angles like snowflakes off headlights gleam, that train whistle fades in the distance like a trumpeter playing *Taps* over an unmarked grave. God, I care too much.

I'm out of pretzels. Don't want another shot of dope. I can smell Jess like magnolias blooming, but can't hold her. My ride's here, I'm leaving. Forget about the milk in the fridge, let it go sour.

*   *   *

A new page. Larry's place at last. A cluttered desk, puzzles, crayons, a deck of cards, trashy gossip magazines, Monopoly. Silk plants that never die, yellow curtains, filthy dirty windows. There's a pretty view beyond the smudge, a country landscape, hills of green. I've got a strong cup of coffee, waiting, just waiting to be let out for a cigarette. Reflections of windows in windows, full of sunlight as if God might walk out of the splash, join me in a cup. It's a nice place this hospital, heaven compared to VA. They got fruit, chips, cookies, no pretzels. I'm the first one up, but here come the others. "Coffee's up." Too many distractions, but I'm not here to write a book. To bad Jess never came here, she might have, it might have saved her. Still, she'd been in plenty of hospitals. I picked the wrong table, there's only two. They're taking blood pressures, temps, keeping me from the page. And here comes the TV, loud, obnoxious. An army of sick people, tired, forlorn, grabbing at Styrofoam cups. Soon we'll get a cigarette, get me some air. I couldn't believe the things Jess was saying about her father, what he'd done. How she'd kept it a secret from me, everyone, even herself.

"Medication!" (pause)

Had 3 cigarettes, enough to make me dizzy, I can breathe again. Just a few sips were enough to get a 9-year- old loaded. He never had intercourse with her, but did everything else. He'd come into her room; wake her up with his touching, feeling her up, his cock in her face. He acts like such a gentleman, a good old dad, but he's a sick, sick, fuck! I need a shower. Again, just to get off this page.

Above the line I'm receptive to change, want to believe in all that is good. This last cup. They lock up my notebook because of its spiral binding, don't want anybody getting hurt, cutting themselves. There are people here who don't have a drug or alcohol problem, who want to kill themselves, who were abused in the worst way and only blame themselves. Seems I've got both ends burning. Do feel as if I'm beginning to emerge out from the bog, realize how my apartment was a prison, a dungeon. I'd bunkered up, my solitary respite an isolation tank of self-loathing just waiting on the hangman's knot. The Blood Man's here to get mine. (pause) Now I can eat something. (pause) Cereal, a small bagel, two bowls, a little cream cheese. (pause) A nice hot shower, brushed the last of my remaining teeth. Don't need my denture here but for eating, I've no vanity left.

*　　　　*　　　　*

Another day. Too much noise in the kitchen, too much TV in the living room. Wait, waiting on a cigarette, the coffee to brew. (pause) Took my pills, had my 3 cigarettes, all the coffee I need to drink. (later) I haven't returned my notebook to the sharps closet. Made a few phone calls, ate some fruit. (pause) Smoked a cigarette. I'm sitting in a reasonably quiet room. *Ring, ringgg,* I don't answer it, there ain't anyone else here, 7 rings before it stops. I don't know what to do with the quiet, but just what I'm doing. Write.

I close my eyes; my body is like a syringe in search of a vein, desperately seeking. I align my legs with my head, my height on the pillow, my breathing in sync like the ticking of a universal clock. I need to hit blood, draw myself up, and find the right spot. I'm off center, realign my legs, open and close my fist, relax, breathe, tick-tock. I keep moving deeper, further away, lost in my own psychosis. "Help! Help! They're gonna kill us!" I awake in a dream's puddle of sweat as if I'd pissed myself. Bad heartburn, feel as woeful as a browning cantaloupe. It's a good thing I'm here, away from the War.

*   *   *

Monday morning. A lot of good that happens like the bad happens without warning, both shit and grace. This here's a happy accident, being here now, how the words do find me. Doctor Gebrane thinks he can help me, knows something about PTSD, has this medication he wants to try. With a thick French accent he gestures enthusiastically, "Gives you new energy, makes you less lethargic, more alert, something the VA doesn't even have. I've had great success treating PTSD with it." I hadn't seen Jess in 30 years, I was gray around the edges, she'd gone completely white like an angel might appear working the gate, just before she introduces you to God. Her voice deeper, groveled by time like a saw-dusted barroom floor, she'd had more spilled on her than one might consume in a lifetime of alcoholism. But she was no poor girl, she had no complaint. Her laugh, her spirit, demeanor, that persevered, you couldn't put a damper on that. I can't write, can't think. I miss my desk, my window view. Too much noise here, too many distractions. Yeah, I know, I'm not here to write.

*   *   *

Haven't been here in a few days. On the page that is. I'm clean 8 days, feeling much better. This new medication is working; I'm awake, more alert, attentive, and alive. Haven't taken any naps. I'll be leaving here in a few days. Thanks to Larry and this place I've got a fresh start, I'm out from under the thumb of it. No, it's not the bottom of the page. No, it's not a filthy dirty window. The smog has lifted, fueled me full of grace. Oh, how I wish I could call Jess and give her the news. Above the line I have no guilt, no future, no past, and no regrets. There's only wind in the trees, leaves of orange and gold, honeysuckle being blown about. I pine for nothing, nothin' I want; like the birds of the field I have what I need. But for Jess. Still, I will not despair. Like water slapping up against the shore, I'm coming into view. I don't know how many more lives I've got, but this one, right here, now, sitting at this kitchen table, I know she'd be happy to see me.

*   *   *

It's criminal how good I feel, like I'd robbed a bank. No, no more guns, no need to riddle myself full of bullet holes anymore. Out from the mine fields like skipping stones, over the bridge, I'm crossing over and won't pass this way again. I've been helping people here. Young men, women, helping them help themselves, pulling 'em out from the mud and the slop, cleaning 'em off, telling 'em it ain't their fault. Sometimes I just listen, that's what they need. I ask questions, try and understand. Surely, I know the hell we impose on ourselves. I'm out from the trenches, seems I've survived.

*　　*　　*

Day 10. Soon I'll be going home. I'm 58 today, but 10 days old. (pause) I've made a few friends here, good people, sick, abandoned souls like me. (later) It's hotter than it ever was, the sun, everything under the sun, we're all gonna melt. It's too hot under my skin, I need to grow fins. Or will it be a nuclear holocaust? Either way, we're gonna melt. You'd better learn how to hold your breath forever, swim underwater. Yeah, we've come full circle; think of it, your great-great-great-grandchildren will be fish. Such is the de-evolution of man. The wind blows me out, into outer space, keeps me cool inside, no virus survives above the line. I run rings around Uranus.

*　　*　　*

It's a blank page, blue lines on a blank page. (pause) Two cups, two cigarettes, it's all I need. Maybe today I'll be leaving. Everyone's hurting, all the girls have been raped, the boys tortured. They'll be up soon, yeah, I'll make another pot. (pause) The light is beginning. I'm awake here, I've gotten the help I need, this is a good hospital. Home, home to my desk, my window view, my music. People here genuinely care, both patients and staff. If! If only I had known about this place before, if only Jess had gotten here. Still, what isn't up to me. I know enough to know I can't fix anyone. (pause) There are a few stories here I need to tell, but not now. I only want to kill all the perpetrators of the world, all those who traumatize the children. That smell, cum, the sweat, I wanna drown 'em in the puke! Sun Tu was sobbing hysterically, Loopahole pulled up his pants, grinning, "You brought her here, now get her the fuck out of here!" It was true, but I didn't rape her. Still, I felt somehow responsible. I would have killed 'im in his sleep, had my bayonet out, but Myles talked me down.

*　　*　　*

Back home! Can't tell the difference between where I am and what I'm writing. Who am I now? Above the line there are no bullet holes, only unmarked fruit trees. I'm drinking coffee, sitting at my desk, I'm happy to be awake. The glass is black but not haunting me. I have faith the sky will rise into view, birds will sing. I owe the Bag Man nothing. Yes, there will be birds, there will be words, and I will be sustained. I'm out of everything but me, but not wasting away. There's money in the bank, and sour milk in the frig. This pen works. I'm quiet in my skin. I'm gonna get a new computer, shop for groceries, see my friends at the morning meeting. I don't have to get fucked up! I will be of service to the page. I will share it all with you. Yeah, I'm all right from my side, right here, right now.

Shay is full of grace, that won't change. I've no bullet holes up my sleeve. 3 butts in the ashtray, and I wish I had a cough drop. I'll pay some bills, need stamps. It's raining, and the drainpipe drips like a metal drum. *Caw, caw, caw!* Coughed up sickly tarred black phlegm on the sleeve of my shirt, gotta quit these cigarettes. (pause) There was a baby born next door, hear it softly crying, heard it's a girl. Cats are running track upstairs, pitter, patter, like elves at work. My hands are on the page. It's all the proof you need. (pause) Again the ashtray is starting over. Do I have to walk in the rain? Is Jess really dead or coming to visit? She sent me a birthday card, two pair of socks, a Ryan Adams CD, *Cold Roses*. About that conversation we had last night. Was it yesterday, or was I only dreaming? She's proud of me for going away, staying clean. I'm not so proud, but grateful. I only asked for help, and got pushed through a window of grace beyond belief. Truly, I say to you, I'm blessed. People at Larry's place were calling me smart. These words are not mine. "I know enough to know I know nothing." I wrote it on the blackboard. It was the last thing I told 'em. I'm just a forlorn scribe who got strung up on a page; I'm the thief on the right. It doesn't hurt any, truth is it feels good. I've got halos round my boot heels. Don't know what time it is, but it's not tomorrow. Time's a funny thing, I'm not really here. Jess ain't dead! Above the line nobody ever dies. It's more than a rainbow, greater than windows, where nothing starts and stops, and weeds flourish in a garden like ripe tomatoes. I'm the weed on the left. This book is writing me. I don't know what I believe in, but what isn't up to me. It's the truth. The drainpipe drips, hurts my ears some, but it's only my flesh that's failing, all that's unimportant. Jess sounded so innocent on the phone last night like a baby softly cries for nourishment, her hair all white, she sent me a picture, she'd be sitting atop Harold's milk truck on a snowy morning, and the clanking of bottles, and all the world applauds. (pause) What will it be like when she gets here? Will it snow before winter comes? Will we recognize ourselves out from the glass, fall in love again? Is it just too damn hot to ever snow again? Are we already in love? Love being timeless like these words, no, you can't take that away. Not this minute, not in an hour, a day, not tomorrow. Shay will always be full of grace, and Maria will follow.

Above the line no one makes tracks in the snow, but angels on a hillside. Or will we two go unnoticed? No, the child will be fed. You see, it doesn't matter, even if they burn all the Jews I'm still a Jew, a scribe, a good soldier. 30 years like 6 million and nothing's changed. Is that Spanish leather, are you secure in your boots? I've been reading this book; everything he tells 'em isn't what they ask. I like it, he's telling the truth. No tricks, no one's right or wrong, no mirrors, gimmicks, sleight of hand. It's the top of the page! Yes, we do love the morning even if we don't love life. We are all like weeds in the night in search of a bird's nest. It's Harlan, I swear, and I'm above the line in the presence of God. Nothing grows taller, but ripe. You will be plucked, plundered, tortured, corned, canned, eaten, and cast out. One ends and another starts up, over and again. (still) Even weeds can fly.

It will settle in your gut and you will know. Know, no one I say can take it from you. Jesus might have said that, or was it Martin Luther King, Jr.? There's no Beast in the black glass, at least it's not who you think it is. You are here among a forest of trees, good and bad pulp. Do not hit the rock with a stick, only ask. I'm a ripe tomato, a kernel of corn under a hot flame, pop, pop, pop. No small arms fire here, I've already done that. There's no paradox, just a pair of ducks, I'm not ducking for cover. Art is born of madness, tossing swine from a cliff, differs from craft in that you must break these chains. (later) A short nap. Helped a kid write his book, a woman get some help for her old man. (pause) Talked to Larry, wants me to write a letter to his boss, encourage her to start a vet's track. It would be a happy alternative to a dysfunctional, misguided VA. Larry's a good man, told 'em so. "Tell Shelia," she's a nurse, "She's the best." Got a story in the mail from my other brother's boy, Brett, another gifted, talented 14-year-old. I'm real excited; there are two aspiring writers in the family. All these years I've been solo, now we are 3. It'll help the cause, we just might be understood. Jess, she'll be here in a matter of days. This ain't the great American novel, it ain't so American. Come to think of it, I don't know shit!

*   *   *

It's early, black glass and demons abound, bad dreams. A cup of my own coffee should help me shake it off. Wake up! I don't remember how much of that dream was real. There's one I have over and again where I'm killing innocents. Wake up felling guilty, bad, but glad to be awake. Didn't talk to Jess last night. Above the line communication is silent, a gesture, a wave of the hand, a mind ripple, smooth like a stone skips across a lake. 3 butts in the ashtray and I'm not here. It's too early for anything but the page. It's too hot for a shirt. Only the refrigerator is running. I need another cup. Wrote that letter to Larry's boss, need a stamp. Need to give Shay a call. I'm in no rush it seems to do anything. I've got pretzels in the house, but need some sugar-free ice cream. I don't think it's raining, don't hear no metal drip. I'm two weeks straight. All I'm trying to do is have a life. Saw to much War footage last night. Not enough sleep. There's no blood in the bathroom. Now if they can only fix my dreams. I can still smell the blood in my dreams. What was that dream? Would like to inspire you to skip smooth stones across frozen lakes like words on a page, or anything you'd like to do, to the best of your ability. Such is grace. Did two meetings yesterday, it helped, but I don't want to live there, where the Big Man growls and never cries.

One thing I highlighted in my letter was the difference between the VA and Larry's place. The lights coming on, the back wood into view. (pause) Had a can of soup for breakfast, split pea with ham. Don't know what clock I'm on. Don't ask. I just write, sleep, eat, and write. See too many doctors, more than I'd like. Since the War I've had 30 or so stays in VA hospitals, from locked psych wards, cancer wards, kidney floors, PTSD programs, TCs, rehabs, and then some. Some stays were good, some real bad, none as good as Larry's place. It's sad if you think about it. A year ago I was in a VA rehab, no detoxification; you had to be 7 days drug free and piss clean to get in. We had this group on grief and loss, I thought, *Good, let's talk about it.* Seemed all the counselor wanted to discuss was grieving your drug of choice. I wanted to talk about the War, my greatest sorrow, lives lost. What made me wanna medicate myself in the first place. She didn't wanna hear it, had her little textbook, had to stick to the game plan. Actually all she had to offer I'd learned in AA, learned it better. Here I was in a VA hospital, a disabled vet, and we couldn't talk about the War. Shame on you! Other combat veterans sided with me, wanted to talk about their trauma. Little Ms. Social Worker got blown off the page. "I don't miss my coke, I miss fuckin' Rodney, and he ain't comin back!" I left, upset, went for a walk.

The next day Dr. Eggo called me into his office. He's the only doctor I've ever met who thinks PTSD isn't chronic. He falsely accused me of saying I wasn't an addict. "That's a lie," I told 'em. Prior to this my counselor was gonna set me up with an outpatient PTSD program that was starting up. Dr. Eggo, it seems, changed his mind for him. Now I was being kicked out, and no further treatment would be recommended. His parting words, "I don't think you'll make it."

When I got home I called my therapist, he'd been contracted by the VA. For the past year I'd been seeing him on a weekly basis. In all fairness I did miss two, maybe 3 sessions. I wasn't showing up for anything but my drugs. He already knew about my discharge, he'd talked to someone at the hospital, said he couldn't help me anymore, and terminated our relationship. His only explanation: I'd missed a few appointments. Now I was grieving the loss of my best friends, an arsenal of weapons, and license to kill! It's a joke. The VA, it's a bad joke. Once you're done soldiering they don't really give a damn. That afternoon I left a message, said he'd helped me, could still, said I was sorry. Left a message the next day, a few days later. No response. See, all us good soldiers are trained to die. If! If you take a bullet, if you're stuck in hell, if you survive, it's your fault. You ain't any good.

*   *   *

Wind chimes, black glass. I believe in wind. Jess called, there are foothills in Idaho. She'll be here in 10 days. The Bag Man called last night, I turned him down. It's too early for music but I wish I had some. Don't know if I'm here, 30 years past, or stuck in a War that just won't end. I think it's raining, ping, ping, flam. I'm off this page, starting over. Above the line we are naked sticks, tree branches in an ocean of dead leaves. The wind chimes 3 beats like wise men bearing gifts. (later) A short nap but full of rest. There's a blue house we could live in. I'm listening to her music, the next song, it's better than the last. Mailed off that letter. There's enough coffee in this brown water. Tomorrow's a new page.

*   *   *

9 days from here. A cold chill, it's me in the black glass spilling words like molasses. I need to take a walk, need a cough drop. I'm not feeling so good; don't know if I want to be awake. I need another cup. I need a phone call. Need somethin'. (pause) Have I told you about my desk? Its round and made of wood, a little larger than a manhole cover, I can fit myself inside it. You can read the lines of bark like time passing, like lines of page, smoke's pouring out. Don't know who won the game last night, I couldn't stay awake. I do think the insurgents are winning the War. It wasn't an important game, doesn't matter who won. If I had a car I'd drive into the woods and never come back, build me a house made of blue branches. Is

Jess only dead, who am I fooling? I turn the page with much apprehension like waves of butter sauce churning in my gut. My toes are jammed up inside these boots. My hair needs cutting. Think I'm gonna puke; throw it all up on a blue line.

Got a new flower for the kitchen table: it's orange and yellow, puffed like baby cheeks. Can I carry your books to and from school? White's nice, I like your hair. I've lost my cowlick. An ambulance screams past, I lose a step. I'm flashin' on a medivac; I've got metal in my leg. I wanna jump, see if I can fly, but they won't let me. On the window ledge is her postcard of a blue house, it's above the line, and happily ever after. No, I haven't any ribbon for your hair. Is Jess only in the ground, blue ash on a black horizon? No! Yes, she's coming, above the grief; she's coming to see me.

Words fall below like sap from bark, syrup into a metal bucket, a large, almost-empty bottle of Listerine on the coffee table. I need to stop this. (later) It's almost Christmas, my cancer's back! Two biopsies tested positive, both my neck and my ear. Should I sing it to the toll collectors? "We wish you a merry Christmas, we wish you—" Fuck it! I'm transferring my notes into this computer. There's snow on the ground but no sign of any milk truck. Where's Jess? Now it's on both sides of my neck like land mines lumped up on a mountain slope. I can't swallow so good, it itches, I can't scratch it. There gonna radiate me Ma, it's my only option. I need the time I guess, time to finish this book. Yeah, I'm just a poor humble scribe.

*   *   *

Words fall below like gold flashing in the pan. Will she recognize me? Will we have to tell each other who we are? Will it matter? Will the past sustain us? Or will we melt under a sweltering sky, the sun too hot for the day like Saul blinded from his horse. Will there be voices? Will there be angels? Will there be ghosts? It's all in the black glass, waiting. (pause) Two butts in the ashtray, the last of this last cup. Above the line we are greater than the day we die, greater than a lifetime. (later) Haven't seen the wrens, maybe they've all gone south. I've been looking for something else, somewhere between Genesis and Eve. Where the page curls and fruit falls from trees like a happy accident, there are no serpents. Where I don't have to ask, and the words just come. I'm not running, but leaving, moving on, where the next page is this one. I've got no time, no one left to lose, not this moment, not you! Won't play that Exodus reel. No sexual ties, no strings attached, no more knots to be undone, without regrets, no guilt, the past is just this.

Went to a writing workshop but there were no writers there, didn't have a voice, but I restrained myself, kept from screaming it out. It's like trying to build a house from wood scraps, without nailing anything down, a lean-to void of truth that won't withstand the storm. That's what I've learned, that it's both sad and tragic. Two people cried, but it wasn't on the page. "She was pathetic," he said it, but never wrote it down, "I was tryin' to be nice." Tom's a bit pathetic, but a good electrician. I'd be the last to have him over, have him watch me wire the house.

"Straight to hell," said the fiery old man, thought he knew God. (pause) Tried Shay, again no answer. It was the hell thing that got me going. Sure, I want out too, but it's hell, and there's nowhere else to go. (pause) Called Jess, left a message. I'm a blue house where death meets the sea. I'm haloed, beating back the devil, ghosts at my heels. There's nothin' more romantic than a blue house, a beached lawn, white trim, a stone path, red leaves falling from the trees. That fence isn't gray, just needs some paint. It's that time of day to sit in a rocker, be in the sun just to feel its warmth. And the porch greets the sky and cloudscapes are for crooning. If! But the page keeps seeping out. Floorboards leak. Words fall below.

Who killed Barbara Allen? If! If this were her blue house, I'd shake off my boots, take off my coat, and be warm inside. But I have no expectations anymore, won't hold a candle dripping wax. Carved that pumpkin out of knot, with my own hands, orange you glad to be alive. Yes! And the dead turn blue like Rodney did, what was left of 'im, but me, I'm turning orange. I'm happy and sad, believing my own lies, pounding back rocks without ever asking, and the drainpipe drips metal bits. It ain't enough to quiet my thoughts, still my thirst. I've got another page to write, one after that. I am the Milk Man, not the Walrus; these are the gates of Harlan. I'll leave it all in the box outside your door. (pause) Jess called. This cigarette fits this cup like a gloved hand. It's just a page, mud and sky. I am your workhorse. See the pretty flowers.

*   *   *

It's the same time a day later; I'm on the clock but not ticking. Nothing but me makes a sound at this hour, but my coughing, not even the heat pipes. Don't know where this chapter ends. It's not despair I'm feeling but something else. I'm excited and afraid. I need a vacuum and a broom, a dead weight to keep my feet on the ground. I'm not fooling anyone with this cough. I'm rust-colored like autumn leaves. Yeah, I'll have another cup. (pause) Sunday morning. Tin cans and balls of string. Cats run track.

I'm surrounded by glass on all sides, don't know which direction is home, don't know where I'm going, don't know anything. Maybe this is despair, under a blanket like mulch, red and orange, worn but still nurturing. I might just eat something and go back to bed. It's just me in the glass, me and my desk lamp. I'm 30 years and 8 days from here. Will I despair when she leaves like Lancelot off mountain tops, jumps off tall buildings over valley streams, hung from barn rafters? Will the sun burn itself up, will we all melt under its thumb? "We didn't fuck down by the creek," she said, "we made love." Thinks she should have brown eyes. Said I was sorry. Maybe it's a girl thing; I need to be more like a girl. Above the line there's refuge from the world, and no army marching bands. I can fit myself inside my desk. I belong here, vanity pressed in a little book like a dead rose tattooed on a snow sled. I'm riding shotgun on Harold's milk truck; I'm all aboard the last train out. Summer's over, bricks not snowflakes fall from the sky, words fall below but can't touch me.

*   *   *

Jess had told me, "On the sick side of the coin, as dirty as it made me feel I had trouble stopping him. It was the love and attention I'd always craved." I wanted her to tell Maria, but she felt she was too young, didn't want to spoil her relationship with her grandfather.

"Why are you protecting your perpetrator?"

"He's old and sickly, can't hurt anyone. I'll tell her when he's dead."

"What about you, when are you going to tell him how he fucked up your life!"

"I don't wanna talk about it anymore." Couldn't help thinking, but didn't say it, at some point Mildred must have thought and said the same thing. That was the end of the conversation. I should have said something more. This last cup is unaware of being last. Beware of thieves in the night. This cough resonates, but I can't put out this cigarette. I've got 6 pills to take, something for pain but I'm not growing any taller. There's no beanstalk coming out of my head. Can't lose myself in reflection, that other living room, that black hole. We flip the page, the timeline, these are not my feet. It's all in this pen point. I'm pouring out like black water. Metal bits fall like scorching rain on a tent roof, and rip through canvas burning a true hole in your gut. It's the truth, yes, without guessing, and we will never touch or see each other again.

It hurts; it hurts all over and again. Like that goldfish to whom you play God, I get 3 flakes of food in my bowl each day. In spite of it all I'm cared for. Moses, 40 fuckin' years, he never got there but saw it from a mountain top, a blue house. It wasn't what he needed anymore like the wind has no windows; no barn door need blow me open and closed. Heaven's like that too I imagine. Above the line we are without sheep. (still morning) There's a glorious sun, this music she sent me lifts my feet off the ground. There's a white railing leading up the path to my blue house, Shay can pull herself along in her wheelchair. If she's having a bad day, Moses gives her push. On a really bad day God sends a limo, the Hunchback of Notre Dame who carries her on his shoulders, and makes her laugh with funny jokes about his hump. "I've got nothin' but love for you now!" The Blue Boy croons.

I had this dream; it's vague, it was good I think. Water splashing up against the rocks, Odysseus landed making bold prints in the sand. This song don't skip, it's written that way, disorder and order in the same beat like the chaos of a madman unchained who might never sit at your dinner table, and only lets Delilah cut his hair. Need a cough drop to quiet my throat. (pause) Tried calling Shay, no answer. There's no sun in her Sunday, it's just another day. They can't leave her alone in bed, she forgets she can't, and tries to walk. She's monitored in the dayroom, propped up in her wheelchair, nodding out to some TV show she cares nothing about. An old woman with Tourette's screams at her stuffed doll, slamming it against the wall, it's stuffing leaking out. It's an old doll, the last of her childhood playthings. Others sit around and drool on themselves only waiting to die. This day like any other day there'll be no visitors for most. At least Shay's got my mom. If she asked me, I'd kill her. Bury her face in a pillow of dream like when we were kids, yeah, I'd kill all the bugs in her room. Off she'd go to my blue house.

*   *   *

I must surrender to the next word, how my strings are pulled. My hands are those of a potato picker. I believe in the wind and how you write me, blow me about like a tall sail ship. This is the land of no promise. A weed has no vanity, is self-sufficient. Above the line the truth is greater than the day. I'm a self-taught log cabin scribe; no ticket, just a hacksaw workin' at these chains. I am the next word! There are no consequences of the gut. I'm not even half free screaming to be fixed like a .50 caliber machine gun bullet whistles in the night, splintering trees into trunks. This is my life's blood. (pause) I'm overwhelmed by the sunset, feel the pain in my lower back, the glass is going black. Again there will be ghosts.

*   *   *

The Bag Man never called me back, that's a good thing. I didn't loose my head in the trash, no blood to clean off the walls, no stench, I don't own a gun. Jess, she's sober these days, will be here in a week, and to think I almost blew it. (pause) Nearly had sex over the phone, she was wet and my line got stiff, "Stop it!" She acquiesced. She reads my last book like me, over and again. It's not yet 4:00 A.M. Tall buildings crash into planes, it's a recurring dream I have, the mud is rising up like pea soup, thick and gooey, I can't move my feet. I don't know who to believe anymore, whose side I'm on. Feel as if I can't make a difference. Am I grateful or at fault, sinking or afloat, dead or being born again? Should I still be in bed dreaming of a better life? Again the ashtray is starting over. I'm coughing up Jesus, white phlegm on a blank page, he don't mind it any. Again I've filled the page with nothin'. (pause) Had an idea for a children's story, a short, stumpy, unwanted weed in a vegetable garden, *The Weedest of Them All*. All the vegetables make fun of him; he doesn't fit and so badly wants to belong. He's so sad, so lonely, but in the end he's plucked up by some birds and along with some blue cellophane becomes part of their nest. Baby birds are born, and to the sweet sound of chirping the weed lives happily ever after. (pause) Again that train whistles off in the distance, down by the river. I can't be writing any children's stories, can't be killing time while splashing holy water at your feet. I'll give it to my friend Nancy, she'll write it good. Do I labor for nothing? (still) Words fall below.

*   *   *

Chapter 5

anticipation must

There is nothing better for a man than to eat and drink and
tell himself that his labor is good. This also I have seen, that
it is from the hand of God. Eccl. 2:24

*   *   *

What a dream I had! I'd fallen on the way in, lay there in the snow,
motionless, still, frozen in time, thought I'd stopped breathing. The
children gathered around me, mumbled prayers, some were crying, slowly
their spirits brought me to my feet, back to life.

"Let them hear you play!" It was the last thing I told the children as
they left the band shelter and walked out into the snowy field making
fresh prints toward the pavilion. Bright lights shown from above, a red full
winter's moon reflected off white earth, a radiant black sky stilled one's mind
of all but the present, puffs of clear steam, alive, gifted, so young, gleaming.
A voice over the PA announced our arrival, "*The Children's Orchestral Blue
Choir of Candor!*" Applause, the waiting crowd stood cheering emphatically.
All of me in a moment's glory as if I'd been stuffed into a tiny glass ball
you'd shake up, snow falling all about me like grace personified, surprise
and joy, wonderment in the eyes of children. Complete, whole, nothing

shy of total perfected brilliance. "Let them hear you play," I said to myself. I was an old gray man fully satisfied with the labor of my teachings. The music and singing began; I broke into a quaint smile and flew upward into the moon's red charm; thus I ascended to God, my Creator.

*　　　　*　　　　*

Had a good therapy session, looked at a car, but I'll never get the financing. I need a phone call, has no one read my last book? Anticipation must wait. Jess will be here in 7 days. The barn side is full of bullet holes, but I've got none up my sleeve. The wind blows me out them little holes into fields of ashen timber. I am delivered. I am a good scribe in service to the word. The page turns and I turn with it. This is just where I started from 30 years later. A circle full of experience, a worn path toward a blue house. I walk this way, talk like this. We know each other's feelings, thoughts, and doings without any words. I've got one last cup, that's it. Need to open a few windows, make up the bed, and visit your side of the street. Don't know what to do first. Don't know how many pages it takes. Is it all in the next word? Anticipate nothing, the page will fill itself. You sir, not I, will tell the story. (pause)

Talked to Charlie, Jess's ex, he's concerned about Maria, she's been too quiet since her mother's death, been keeping to herself, not seeing her friends. Big Charlie's a good dad, has a new wife, works hard making beautiful furniture, he made this desk. Gotta get at the truth, wheel it out front, center stage, and make you look. What and who killed Barbara Allen? (pause) I ain't slick, my hair ain't greased, and I wear no rings, trinkets, no eyeliner. I've blackened both sides of the bathroom mirror. Had enough of shooting myself up, down. Now you see my arms have healed, and the light hits the back wood just as it should. These damaged goods, the sustenance of my labor, the hole you must go through won't fit a red-tailed hawk. It's safe inside my blue house. Dear friend, I do so anticipate your read. We are all waifs, the sons and daughters of Moses, children in a handbasket among the marshes, tall reeds of the Nile. We are the guardians of Babylon.

*　　　　*　　　　*

I'm up with the sky and out from the glass. Don't know how many days I'm clean, but she'll be here in 6. And the lamp stand rattles, mettle shards, steaming flesh, gaping wounds. Does she want to dig it all up? They're picking up the trash, *beep, beeping*, backing up. Don't know if I can do it,

I don't remember doing what she says I did. *Beeping*, can't be backing up so much, is it all I'm doing here? No, I don't do those things anymore. Do I rush out to a meeting, or keep to the page? I don't think it was me who scared you that way; something must have happened before me, why hasn't she gotten over it? Was to find out it was all about Jack. Fuckin' Jack! These are not the foothills of Idaho, but the bedrock of Mount Sinai. I see us far off in the distance in a garden of fig trees. Don't know if I'll get there, but keep moving. It's a big ball of tears, greater than me. Don't know how many more pages before I rest. I've got this desert between my toes, an unquenched thirst. I will ask, and the rocks will cry like a waterfall, show me the way, put words on the page. I know nothing of sand castles, only sandbags, and bunkers full of secrets that must be exposed. (pause) Geese passing, I can hear the flap of their wings if I remain perfectly still. I can hear the wind. It's too early for music but not for this. I should eat something. (pause) Leaves are falling; the heat pipes are coughing. It would be so much easier just to quit. I've got cancer all over my neck, new lumps cropping up daily. Ma, I'll be starting up radiation in a week or two, they're gonna make me glow like Rudolf's nose. I need to hit the bank, clear the ashtray, collect my things, put some order to this place. One shot would take it all away, but I can't be killing me anymore. I need a phone call, something to get me over the top, out from between, and into the present tense. I can't rely on yesterday's words. Jess is dead, ain't comin' back, it's just me filling in the holes. I don't believe in anything anymore, only these words as you might find me here, and that pen just died. My family doesn't understand, don't get it at all, no, they find me guilty, can't comprehend the horrors of War! And the wind chimes. Dear Mom, You're the reason I left, I couldn't be your mountain. I need that car so I can drive far away from here where the promise isn't tainted, and the past ain't pulling at my heart strings. Above the line there's only love, no trash, no garbage trucks. To be like a tree, the gift of wind, the call of the rocks, home again. This last cup doesn't know it's last until it's over like a book of pages, like a heartattack. God, this is no hoot. (pause) Tried calling Shay, again no answer, where's my best friend? My blue house has been washed out to sea. Above the line there are no homes, only blue space. I'm knotting up, turning orange. The ashtray is full. Yeah, I've nowhere else but here. I'm spilling over; tryin' to get to the bottom of it, Jack's bucket, Jill's dead, and it's a hot sun I'm pissing on, greater than the day, hotter than it ever was. This cancer will not have its way with me, not until I'm out of words. I've got a new pen with a finer point. Won't stab myself but once, not yet, not in the presence of God. I've had enough of sand, desert sun, and canned goods. I want to point back at you, but it's only me in the glass. Where the fuck is Myles? I'll have one more cup, make the bed. No, you couldn't love your mother good enough, couldn't satisfy her lack of self. She'd always be screaming for more, more was never enough. She'd make us line up, my aunt's 5 boys and the 5 of us. If you didn't hug and kiss her good enough you had to do it again. Over and again. She smelled like overripe rotting fruit. Her family, Hungarian Jews, were all killed by the Nazis, her Mongoloid sister they even killed twice. On Christmas she'd come for dinner having already eaten at the Salvation Army, she'd have shopping bags full of clothes she'd collected on the street. I got a brown and yellow scarf that came down to my knees, tripped me up. Once when I was 8, my mother was on the phone with her crying, "I do love you, Momma, I do!" I picked up the upstairs phone, "You stop making my mother cry!" Grandma Szabo stepped off a city street corner one bright fine day, was hit by a garbage truck, and got crushed dead. The driver didn't see her; the sun was in his eyes. She lived in a rat-infested apartment; they later found all this money under her mattress. One Christmas we were lined up for hugs and kisses. I was suffocating from the War, Jess had left me, and I was pining away. When we were kids she'd make me and Shay watch Oral Roberts, "Heal, heal," than we got to watch wrestling, Wild Man Frogo was our hero. After the second hug Grandma said, "Don't worry, you'll find God." I went into the bathroom, looked at myself in the mirror; I had this pale death look about me. Saw Rodney in the glass, cut in two, a torso like his, a face like mine. I cried like an abandoned child given up at birth. It was me, me who wandered off. (pause) "Don't put your able on the table." When Grandma said that, meaning elbow, me and Shay would always laugh. Life was that simple.

If! Don't ask, I cracked my stick against the rock. Betty's a land mine; she'll only leave you broken in two and bleeding out. (pause) Someone called about reviewing my book. Don's got cancer, listened to his choices, and made a few suggestions, "Yeah, a support group helps." All I need each day is a page, a few flakes in my bowl. All I know about God is it's not a wind of my own making. (later) Saw Jacob in town, the young writer I helped with his story. He came to cash his check, get a cheeseburger and a coke. His girlfriend wore a big metal cover across her chest, said manhole, just had to laugh. Had a nap, but no dreams of heavenly brilliance, no blue icicles glistening from rooftops. Now I ask, where has all my love gone? Again to vacuum up the crumbs of a spilled pretzel bin, need to stop eating pretzels in the dark. (pause) I can only play what the wind says. I've got more holes in me than bullets in a gun. I whistle while I work, shoot first, ask no questions, don't ever question the wind. Don't need this fuckin' guilt, remorse, it's useless. I'm all dead inside like an empty barn that once was a manger. Is this where Jesus was born, how long's that donkey been nailed to the wall? I had this goldfish once; it was a birthday gift I didn't want. It got 3 flakes a day, but knew nothing about me, or where them flakes came from. That goldfish taught me everything I know about God. It died and I flushed it down the toilet. It's whatever you do with my body, but flush 3 times. All God wants of me is to fill the page. (pause) Jess confessed, "After our phone conversation I tore off my pants, jumped into bed and had sex with you!" I did the same thing today, but her flesh is all gone now, can't smell them magnolias, or feel the arch of her foot so pronounced against my flat feet. Need a cough drop. Nothing came in the mail, no phone calls. I need another cup. I owe the bank, and the bank owns me. All that's keeping me alive is this page. What was so good yesterday is broken now. Like he said, "No, nothing works that hasn't been broken." I'm en route to the junkyard. That last book about the dead and the dying. And the dead have died for nothing. Up against the outer wall, motherfucker! Can't hop no train anymore, I'm too old for the highway. Don't know any waitresses in Cheyenne, stone merchants in Old Bisbee, gun slingers in Tombstone. I miss living on the open road, hopping boarders with Geronimo. Is it all lost in the black glass anymore, like I miss playing ball, or the vibrant exuberance of falling in love? This page is all that's left me here. I'd like to be Picasso, or the hand of God if only for a moment. I'd like to rip out Jack's heart with a screwdriver, staple his lips to his asshole, his butt to a bumper, pretend I'm a dump truck, back him into the Great Wall of Mirrors, again, over and again. God, the sun's too damn hot. No, I can't dig up her bones, put her back together again. God, I'm old, can't be wielding a pickax. Like all the King's horses, these blinders got me believing my own lies. And Mother Goose told the truth, and Grandma Szabo pulled at our toes, "And this little piggy," like swine from a cliff. God, it's all only mud and sky. You can't go home, there's no blue house. And all the King's madmen go wee, wee, wee, wee into puddles of spilled milk down the pant of my leg. That's all that's left of Mother Goose, guilted in the black glass, who should have left you years ago, but she had other kids to feed. Poor old Mother Goose like that lady in a shoe, and we've got one last cup to get it right. (pause) Super chunk peanut butter, two slices of bread. Should do some laundry. (later) The bed it's made, clean sheets, my hands and feet. I don't really want to be awake. Saw Henry Miller in the bookstore but couldn't get a read on him; some people say we look alike, don't know, had my eyes closed. Found a new lump in my throat, it's getting harder to swallow. This desert needs to rise up and swim. Yeah, a liquid diet, maybe a tube for feeding. If! If I had a 3rd eye it would be a bullet between the next word and this one. 3 butts in the ashtray, Abraham, Isaac, and an Unholy Ghost. My friend Ed, my roommate at Larry's place, he'd been tortured, also took the beatings for his little brother, but his brother don't remember that, tells Ed, "I never had a big brother." The nerve of the little prick! (pause) Don't know how long this page will last, as long as this cup I guess, until the words run out. Me and Ed were the best of roommates, he kissed me when I left, but like Myles I'll never see him again. It's all too sad, all of us. Andrea was raped by her Uncle Fred when she 10, told her momma who didn't believe her. It was just her imagination, she was always making shit up, no one believed her. Andrea was made to apologize for all her false accusations. At the age of 16 she ran away from home, but Uncle Fred followed her halfway across the country, raped her again. Andrea got pregnant; Uncle Fred took away the baby. (pause) God, she's dead in her flesh anymore, like Shay Full of Grace, she can't move a muscle. Some 30 years later, and Andrea's never seen her daughter. Uncle Fred, he keeps all his dirty little secrets in a music box, plays her daughter softly to sleep, sleeps with her, and she believes it when he tells her, "Your momma's dead."

Where's he live? I'd like to be the hand of God! (pause) Just had to beep the Bag Man, stop these thoughts beeping me back, back into knots. I'm laid out on these tracks, stuck in the mud, splinters and floorboards, rockets and mortars crashing all around me. God, ain't there nothin' to be done about it? What's getting closer, it's in my lap, ears bleed, and it rips the fuckin' buttons off my shirt. I can smell the gun powder like a bloodhound on blood, there ain't nothin' I can do but own it. If! If I were the hand of God.

If I dig any deeper I'll be in China. Jess is dead, there's no way around that. (pause) None of the men at the meeting heard me, just bounced off some rhetoric void of practice, words without knowing. You've got a stiff upper lip, a mouth full of Astroturf, hearts bound in bootstraps, not a word was felt. All you need is a loaded gut to cut off these feelings of the heart. If Jesus died for our sins, why the knife at my throat? Why the rope? I can't skip stones, jump no more. And Smyth, he's one with the sun and the rafters. Who will cut him down? When you're dead they tell lies about you, "What a good soldier he was." And up against the outer wall. Now you must walk the path between the lines, shut up, motherfucker, and read! Again I had to leave. This sadness, all this sadness about me. (pause) Called Shay, called her "Grandma," but she didn't remember who she was. Jess is free; me and Shay are dead in the flesh. I'd like to leave you here. Above the line where all's forgotten. Won't someone shoot me full of grace? I can't remember how to button my shirt, tie my shoe, undo that knot. The sun is out, and all these ghosts are looking back at me. I hate this shit, there's no railing to hold on to, I hit the keys with a vengeance, and only the black glass has any hint of compassion. The dead understand and are beckoning me, *come home*. This rash on my ear, it's cancer too; I've got a throat full of jungle rot, just dying to meet you, see all my dead friends again. The moon is red, all my socks have holes like moons, and the wind passes through me like a tunnel mountain pass, bullets and buttons, tall buildings collapse. My vision goes soft on the sides, lighting and thunderbolts. I've no fight left. (pause) Put on some socks anyway. Dogs barking on the left side of my brain, shooting sparks, my right arm goes numb, I can't feel what I'm writing like you can't see me. I'm a solid black line, flip the page, but I don't know what page it is. I wish he'd get here like the hand of God, knock me off my horse. I don't believe in nothin' but wind. Tell me, what is it they don't understand? And how many more pages before it stops me?

God needs love. Again I'm coughing up Jesus. "Let them hear you play!" But the children like the dead poets have all been molested. The music stops. It's only me here scratching at my fleshy goose self.

* * *

The refrigerator makes a noise like monkey chatter. My chest feels heavy just above my heart. The Bag Man cancelled, couldn't find no product. To my benefit, I guess. Not a bad night's sleep, but there were too many dead bodies to count. Gotta get this computer running, put this here in type, edit these notes. Jess will be here in 5 days, again to think I almost blew it. 30 years, and I don't know if I can open the door, seems I already have. Yesterday was a good day with the pen, today it doesn't matter. What we all need is some good news, a good play on a windy stick. The heat's coming up. Above the line there's no need for escape, no body bags, no product. The glass is black, do I labor for nothing? It's all in how you make the bed, not a matter of thread count. Everybody takes a bullet. (pause) I'm only waiting on the snows to cover my naked limbs, to ride again with Harold on his milk truck. I can hear Shay moaning in her sleep, she can't even turn herself so to ease her discomfort. I'll do the morning meeting. (pause) I met a guy on my walk named Joe; he lives here in this complex. He's 66, has 10 grandchildren, a daughter in Baltimore. "It was 96 there last week, and humid."

"Yeah, the sun's hotter than it ever was."

"It's scary." He's from Boston, bikes and walks a lot, looks terrific for his age.

"It's a beautiful morning."

"Yeah, even if it's scary."

"Can't help but enjoy it."

This ain't any church, it's a church basement, here there are no graven images. Unlike the people upstairs we each have our own God. I tell 'em mine's a Goldfish; I get 3 flakes a day. Still, there are some stone cold idol worshipers who'd like to tell you what to believe. I'm grateful I don't have to believe 'em. The heat pipes have fallen off the wall, the windows are curtain less, but the light is warm. There's a power surge in grouping greater than you, than I'll ever be, surely it's the hand of God.

Dust collects on bookshelves like hair on your chin, blows out the same old rhetoric, that same bad prose. You don't have to tell me your name twice, to begin and end with Mike. You're dangerous, imposing your interpretation, your will on others as if you were the right hand of God. God is ambidextrous, eats with his fingers, and loves raw fish. We need to take this stuff off the page and put it to practice. Truth is an excavation, changes from moment to moment, day to day. I might not believe me tomorrow. What's past is present; you need not make the same mistakes again. This is an archeological dig. I've no comment about your book even if I don't believe you. My name ain't Mike. I'm grateful. (pause) That nice woman who stutters just said what I came here for, "Truth is I wanna get lo... loaded!" (later) Something of a nap, I don't think I slept. All these birds have gathered on the branches of my loveseat, red and blue. My dreams are of steel girders that bend in the wind like geese flap. No mail, no phone calls. Need to get out for awhile, off the page. Need to hit the bank, I'd like to hold it hostage, pay the mortgage, save the farm. Need cigarettes. It's too damn hot, October ain't what it was. Jess called, she's leaving tomorrow, she'll spend a few days on the Island visiting family before coming north. Need to call the Bag Man and cancel my order. It's 30 years later; we won't be hooting it up any. God, I'm scared, I've been alone here so long that I don't know how to act.

Heard Ed left the hospital, should be hearing from him soon. We've both got metal in our legs that hasn't yet worked its way to the surface. In the beginning Ed had trouble getting out of bed, took him a week to take a shower. He's a nice man, a good man, all boxed up, a tortured soul in a troubled state of mind. He's on some new meds now, heard he's doing better. Again the sun's going out; I'm only tired, worn through, still at War with myself. I could die for my thoughts, the thrill of it all like a Cracker Jack box surprise. I'm almost dead here, pictured in the black glass, rushing in my veins and heart like a prize fighter, ring, ring that fucking bell! Going up, down! The hand of God set on fully automatic, rifle tightly strapped across my forearm, sweaty palms, and a finger on the trigger. I'm punch drunk insane, come out from abandoned buildings, blasting! I love the power like the son of Jesus come down from the cross; come to avenge my father's death. It's the perpetrators I want, I'm gonna kill 'em all and raise the dead back to life! (pause)

That cough made me dizzy. "God bless you." Again someone thinks I've sneezed, happens all the time. "Think you've got the wrong number."

*   *   *

20 days clean, God is looking out for me, keeping my head below the sandbag line, out of range. Black glass, cats running track. We're the only ones alive at this hour, them and the page. Now if he shows up here, the Bag Man with his bag of shit, give me the strength to chase him away. I've got my own black bodybag I'm toting around; it's a heavy enough burden for any one man. Jess is leaving Santa Cruz today; she'll be here in 4 days. Need to call the VA, see if they can get me this new medication of Doctor Gebrane's. I need to fill out the forms for a $180.00 computer rebate. Why not just give it to you in the first place? I hate paperwork, but not that much. Some people won't bother, more money for Office Depot, a polite form of thievery. The lottery, it's a poor people's tax, and where have all the educational benefits gone? Is no child left behind, do they all have computers, or did they spend their milk money on cigarettes and beer? Don't really know if I want to be awake for this.

Another cup. 3 butts in the ashtray. It's not this cigarette I'm smoking but the next one. It's too early for birds, they're asleep in my blue house, nestled in among the *Weedest of Them All*, wait, waiting on a blue sky. I hope Ed calls me before he shoots any dope. (pause) The cats are quiet, no train whistle off in the distance, no wind chimes. A long look in the bathroom mirror, it's not vanity I'm looking for, it's another lump in my throat. God, what a bust! Just when I was feeling good about myself. There are no dishes in the sink, no geese flying past, daylight hasn't been saved, it's more than an hour from here. See, it's all about this page, that's how I want it to be. Hold me, please. (pause)

I can spit ink into the fire and make the flames go higher, bounce words up high off a stone wall, and make handbasket catches like say hey, Willie Mays into this old beat-up glove of Dad's. I can write whatever fate is served up, and tell the truth. Above the line there are only words of truth, and nothing is greater than the page.

Go figure, what isn't up to me, but some kid somewhere might be reading my last book, he might be saying to himself, *I don't ever wanna be a soldier.* Again to make the bed. Just to feel like Job on a good day, is something to be grateful for. (pause) Yeah, I might be listening for the wind, my arms unfurled like clean sheets, still the wind makes no noise of its own, but blows them sheets dry. The sun's too hot, and the rains can't put it out. Now any sort of breeze seems gentle. I pray silently on the page, the trees don't move, and no wind chimes. It's a cold barren sky, still a full moon glows orange in hopes of being saved. I'm no wiser than the fool, and won't tell you what to believe. I've got one last cup to blow it all out into, another round of you. (pause) The bed is made to the best of my ability. These lumps make me nervous, they're not shrinking any. Jess is coming soon. Don't hear any drainpipe dripping, that metal annoyance pinging off tin roofs. Ain't any Triggers here but for Roy's horse. This pen works. There's no dust on my bookshelves. (pause) This cough drop will surely quiet my cough, I'll put some ChapStick on my lips and seal up the cracks. Why is it I so need to fill the page, another, and another after that and it's never good enough, or if it is, it won't sustain me. There seems no respite. Why is it? And your blue house eludes me. God, is it all too late for love? That last book is finished, but it seems I'm never done. Above the line is always post-bottom, followed by a line, and others follow. It all gives me a headache, all this breathing. I'm a leafless tree naked before the wind, waiting on the snows, to ride shotgun once again on Harold's milk wagon. He'd always say, "If it weren't for me there'd be no breakfast table, no milk for cereal, coffee or tea, and no butter for your bread." It filled me with purpose like words bring life to black glass. There's an eternity there in your milk box. Two quarts and a stick of butter for Mrs. Tishbin. Me and Harold like a tall sail ship on a starry morning flight, like wings on the heels of a snowflake. "This also I have seen that it is from the hand of God."

There's that train whistle calling that runs along the rivers bank, winds and stops, "All aboard." It's the last train out; no one knows this but me. No one cares that I'm leaving. When it's your turn you'll see me, take thought of all the dearly departed. I'd like to be a tugboat, take you upriver where you're needed most. I'm almost off this page, and you've only just found me. I've got more pills to take, two shots of air. These holes in the old red barn, it's how the light finds me the way. Me, you, all of us, we're just waiting our turn. That was my last sip. (pause) I'm empty now, the ashtray is clear. Still, black, no view beyond the glass. This is all that God wants of me, what I'm doing here, this page.

Shay doesn't need to read this; she already understands what we all need is a shot of grace. Need to brush my teeth; I'll eat a banana first. Don't wanna loose these 6 beautiful teeth of mine. I'm most at home on the page like a jet fighter plane without a cloud in the sky. This medication helps. I can turn on the shower and step inside, I don't have to stand there and wait anymore, not knowing what to do next. Who, who's next? Who will I meet on my walk today? There are angels among us strangers; this too I believe is from the hand of God.

It's a beautiful morning, even if it's already too hot. (pause) Sitting on these church steps waiting for someone to open the door. The Big Man just pulled up, he's got a key, "Good morning." Saw the Thin Old Lady on my walk, she smiled and waved from across the street; she wore green today, a black hat, in contrast to her dog's blue eyes. Walked under the sparrow tree where the bird shit hits the pavement like wedding rice, you already know that. The News Man walks past, I glance but don't look up, he's determined in his gait to get home and read. Me, I'm working on this yellow sheet. An old orange Porsche pulls out of a neighbors driveway, I just have to look.

"Hi, Charlie."

"Supposed to hit 94 degrees today."

"Terrific!" (pause)

I'm not happy, joyous, and free like the speaker talks about, never will be I guess. I'm just here so I don't get loaded. Yeah, I have no expectations, this is a church basement, be grateful I don't sing in the choir. I know the likes of hell, both inflicted upon and self-imposed, and this here is better than a bootstrap. Can't lash at my own skin, or be my own master. (pause) Just told the group, "I don't come here to sound good," revealed all my insane thinking. Mike thinks he's a real alcoholic, the only one among us, as if there was a distinction to be made. I say to you, no one comes through these doors feeling good about oneself. No, I'm not here for the coffee and donuts, Donna's homemade breads and pies. And the women, they're all sick and unavailable like me. Still, anyone with any doubt, Mike just sent them reeling for a fix.

(later) A nap. We were flipping cigarettes through the air, burning furniture, curtains, scratching couch covers with ballpoint pens, pissing in the waste basket. I was trying to talk him out of being a wise guy. "Keep pushing them all away, you're different, yeah; see how good that makes you feel." That's all I remember of the dream; still, we all know how it ends, empty and forlorn.

Jess is overhead, somewhere in flight. I can't stop listening to the music she sent me. No phone calls, no mail. It's a hot, sticky afternoon; I'm stuck under a hazy gray sky that's scratching at my throat. Mike, he's dangerous, the way he takes charge, walks 'em out the door. Why not tell us about your kids, yeah, you know, the ones that haven't talked to you since you don't remember when? This here, it's all about healing, making people feel welcome, filling in them holes we'd rather crawl down into. Mike missed that part in the literature, somewhere after kindergarten and the Fourth

Edition of the Fat Book. 3 butts in the ashtray, I'm feeling thick like a rain-swelled forest, like a gun with a blood clot about to burst. Again to make the bed, put out the trash, and again, I will make more garbage, smoke another cigarette, and fuel these lumps. (pause) Doctor Lubin called, wants me to come up to New Haven and talk about my book.

(again) It's almost like rain, slick as an oil spill it slips from my hand. Are there no tree trunks to huddle up against, no angels in the saw dust? I only want to shoot my gun.

Saw John on my walk, he was too drunk for conversation, angry, lost, it's everybody else's fault. He reeked like Dead Sea silt, don't know why he had a toothbrush in his pocket, forgot to tie his shoes, his lawyer papers falling out of their folders to the ground. His old Mercedes had a few new scrapes and dents; at least he made it home, pray he didn't kill anyone. "Lincoln had ships in Charleston, wanted to send 'em back to Africa." John liked my last book, wants to read this one.

"You'll be dead before I'm finished, the gout, your liver; your wife wants to push you down the stairs." She pulls into the driveway, "She's gonna run you over!" Made him laugh. She wears a frown, they don't speak, and she hurries into the house. And me, I'm no better or less, nothing else to say. All his kids have grown up, left him, he's selling his house. Me, I don't own one.

He screams at me as I walk off, "It's all about the money!"

And how will we look each other in the eye, me pickled in time, she a healthy nut. The back wood is motionless, no birds. I've got one last cup, a smooth, flat stone I'm thumbing to death. Didn't do a thing today other than this page I'm on. I've stopped counting; I've no skill with numbers. There's no movie I'm seeing, I know them all, and how they end. Can't watch the news, don't need another weather report. The next War might be the last. Who's first to shoot? Who's got the nukes? Who's next will be the last to know. It's a wasteland, a sad beautiful love song that knows the time of day. The hour is late. I really don't want to be here anymore. Don't wanna roll up my sleeves, pull up on these boot straps. Yeah, I'll just slip into this hole and disappear. (pause) Mom called, "Joey Bishop died today."

"Didn't know he was still alive."

The only news worth reading is on the sports page. I can make the bed without pulling off the sheets, swallow the ashtray and save on cigarette money. I need a new-found providence, a platter full of ribbon and grace, garnished in top soil. Haven't heard from Ed, wish I had his number, hope he's not shooting dope, being beaten by his dead abusive father. I know where Abraham took Isaac, and he had to pay, and pay, and pay. How many more bullet holes? My mom's too old for me to say it, but she still thinks she knows best. She's no real danger these days, a lot like Jack; besides, no one fucks me up better than I do. (stop) That was my last sip, which way is off this page? Rinse and clear, but tomorrow's the same old page, over, over and again. (pause) No dirty dishes in the sink. Them 6 o'clock church bells, a bad recording of *Ode to Joy*. Why does everything end like this? And the sun goes out. What must I do? How does one live above the line? What to believe anymore?

*   *   *

I can't get me off the page. 3 weeks clean, but it ain't me who's doing it. Trying to fit myself into a routine. I've got the morning meeting and this book I'm writing. All I've really got is this page, this hole I'm working my way out of. A head full of black glass. Still, I'm grateful, all my bills are paid, and I owe the Bag Man nothing. Jess will be here in 3 days. Not a bad night's sleep, don't remember any dreams. Nothing scary. The coffee's good. Two butts in the ashtray. I need to blow my nose. (pause) The heat is coming up. My back hurts. Looked in the mirror, think my lump's growing. Splashed some water on my face, still orange. My hair's electrically charged, untamed like Einstein's, but not so white, not so friendly. I need to socialize, meet some other lumps. Jess is on the Island with Maria, won't get to meet her this time, she's goin' to visit her dad, Big Charlie. Leaves are peeking orange and gold, proudly announcing her arrival, still nothing exists at this hour beyond the black glass. It's only me looking back at myself. No, I'm not overly excited; anticipate only what will be trees, birds, and a view outside the glass.

It's been 30 years. Almost everything's changed. All that we've learned since, still, what we've always known hasn't changed. And what I don't know, see, I get these 3 flakes in my fishbowl each day. Keeps me guessing. I know enough to know I know nothing. The memory lives in the black glass. The past is in the present tense, the ghost of our lives. Again I've filled the page with nothin'. Could use some wind, move me down the line. (pause) Go ahead, you can retrace your steps, but can't change the outcome. Jess is dead! Cats are running track on the floor above, the ceiling snores. Its 5:00 AM, all is black, but for this lamp. Too much heat comin' up, feel sick to my stomach. Start the ashtray over, open a window. Kill all the windows, let her be dead. No! Anticipation must prevail. I'm waiting for nothing, only filling the page, only waiting to die. I'm just like all the rest, I guess, afraid. This coffee isn't working, making me feel any less dead inside. I've got all her postcards lined up on the windowsill. There's enough smoke in here to be the Jersey Turnpike. Anticipation is accumulative then it bursts like a dam. I've got a trigger finger on the heart of the wound, quenched in disbelief. She called from the airport, left a message, "I'll be seeing you soon." Is it a matter of days or weeks? I had a year to do in Nam, a page to fill, but it never ends. When she gets here I'll have nothing more to wait on. What to say? Will she rise up from the dead like Lazarus, or will I self-destruct, burst into flames and go the way of milk wagons? Down by the river where death greets the sea the wind blows hollow like a train whistle off track. I anticipate nowhere as my resting place. This too is from the hand of God. (pause) This last half a cup, another cigarette, throat drop, please. All my good mornings are on the page, this one too. Still, I anticipate a view outside myself, when the black glass becomes clear and black-capped chickadees will circle my head like a warm bowl of porridge. I'm sitting on a loveseat made of tree branches. I'd love it if it rocked. I'm an American Indian at heart. I'm the paper ring from a cheap cigar my grandfather once smoked. My hands are like his. Yeah, all I anticipate anymore is zero, where nothing is defined. "We're all refuges," he told my mom and sent her off to secretary school. She was the smart one. I'm just a stone's throw away, skipping stones across the lake. It's this page I'm on. (pause) And who will I encounter on my walk today? Yes, I do believe there are angels in the woodwork.

Someone on my walk says, "There's rain in the forecast."

"Good, we need the rain."

"Shouldn't hurt us any." (pause)

"And when the dream becomes so solidified that it has to be taken to the stage of reality, then you'll see stone." *Bob Dylan*

It's who I am, why the past is present tense, makes sense, why we skip stones. And Shay is full of grace. I like these church steps. I've got no one else here to talk with. Did walk under the sparrow tree, did say, "Good morning," fortunately I wasn't hit with any wedding rice.

"Summer's back," says The News Walker, shrugs his shoulders.

"It's only gonna get worse." We agree on the weather, Man's molestation of Earth, gives us something to talk about.

"Stay cool."

Once inside the air gets cooler, it's one good thing about being in a basement. We read half the time, what I've already read. Mike believes everything he needed to learn he learned in kindergarten, some book he read, trouble is he hasn't learned anything since. Goes into his spiel again about being a real alcoholic. Romulus is coming unglued, whispers to me, "He's scary." I can't restrain myself, somebody's gotta stop 'im. I get my hand up.

"Nobody comes through these doors feeling good about themselves. A rose, is a rose, is a rose, is a drunk, believe it! Gertrude Stein said somethin' like that." I should have kept my mouth shut; it just feeds his shit when he knows he pisses people off.

(later) Jess called, she's shopping with her mother, her two bleached-blonde nieces, Faith and Hope, and Maria Full of Grace. (pause) Someone called from Barnes and Noble, I've got a reading in January. It looks like rain, it feels like August, the bed's unmade, and the ashtray is full. Jess remembers, I don't, says I talked of having 3 personalities, one that wanted to kill her, one that was madly in love with her, and another being indifferent. One was named LaFarge, she doesn't remember which one. I recollect the name, heard it before, but that's all I remember. (pause) I know she was afraid of me, I do know how much in love we were. Don't know who or what killed her. Said I was sorry.

If! If one experiences anything, the past is present in everything you do. Took a drive away from here, ate a big lunch. A trickle, a tear, but what we need is a hard rain. If the Bag Man called I'd cave into that hole, cry real tears. (pause) Made some phone calls, Laura finished the book. "Brilliant," she says. Don't know if I believe her, it's this book I'm writing. Anyway, I'm just a scribe. Above the line it's about showing up, God does all the work. This heat makes me angry; it's a soft rain on a hard shell. 3 weeks clean and I'm ready to shoot myself dead. (pause) Ed called; he's a clean man, a good man, an inspiration. At this moment I don't need a fix.

*   *   *

Too early, but what does time matter? I'm these many pages without counting; she's two days from here. I'm another day further away, but can't escape the past. Sure, I could buy it all back with a shot, a soup spoon full of dope, hell in a handbasket. I'd be back in a War of my own making. I'd be less than a ghost, the walking dead. Don't remember what dreams. (pause) It's raining, the sound of my favorite metal drainpipe drip, and the shadow of a loveseat. I do believe what she says I did. And what will we do when she gets here? I feel like a tall sail ship coming into port, but I've been away too long at sea, don't remember how to act. Yeah, like I'm lost, anticipating being home, but I don't know where, what home should be. I'll have another cup, fill the bottom up. (pause) Got a new flower for the kitchen table, purple, a hint of red, *ping, ping, ping, tick-tock*. It's not yet 4 o'clock. It's cool enough with the sliding glass doors open, limits what ghostly activity. I'm excited enough about her coming, need these two days to ground myself. Thinking she'll be here soon, is keeping me clean, don't wanna fuck this up. I'd like to blast some music, songs she sent me, but it's too early. Just this page, it's never too early, or late for this. When she gets here might we dance on the graves of who we once were, or will we fall desperately into the pit? There's that train whistle, down by the river, so faint, distant, so far off anymore. And the wind howls underground through the bones of her decaying flesh. The drip, dripping metal *tings, pings* of the drainpipe like pangs to the heart. My friends the crickets, bleeding through the cracks, nestled softly in the backwoods. *Caw, caw, caw!* "God bless me." (pause) That cough just spilled me out of consciousness. Anticipation is like a polished fork waiting on a big thick slice of black heavenly pie. There's no spoon in the bathroom, blood smells emanating out from last night's debacle. I'm feeling grateful like a netted fish spread bountifully over the crowd. I've got coffee, bread, cigarettes, milk, I'm moving forward down the page, above the line as the words do find (define) me here. I anticipate a great orchestral blue choir. I do believe in the day. Empty the ashtray, start it up all over again. Yeah, I'll have another cup. Should I get a haircut so I look pretty for when she gets here, maybe just a trim? I've been getting through, might I start living? I'm a cool duck on an icy pond, upstream, above the line. Ain't nobody awake at this hour, it's just God, me, and them crickets. What's good is I'm not so busy in my head, not lost in the bathroom mirror. See, I get these 3 flakes in my bowl each day like wise men on the page; it's like opening gifts on Christmas morning. I don't know how far I've traveled to get here, what I did or didn't do. Truly, I am not worthy. What isn't up to me, I know, but the music's playin' nice right here, right now, a sweet refrain. (pause) Anticipation must, but I never anticipated good stuff.

I lived in a log cabin on the Lake of the Woods, we never knew what drugs the other was on, but we stayed fucked up, drunk. She left that night crying, scared for her life, afraid of that part of me that wanted to kill her, wanted her dead. The back wood was all black, black like glass, ink, like a mountain lion's cave, void of moon and starlight. She tripped, fell in the mud, frantic, couldn't find her way up, slipped, and couldn't get out from the bog. Heard footsteps, but it wasn't me, I wasn't in pursuit. I'd only been back a year from the War, but she knew nothing of that. Was still at War I guess, but unaware of it, never said nothin' to anyone about it. I would never run blindly into the jungle. I'd secured the perimeter with barbed wire, claymores, trip flares, there were landmines the French had left behind, didn't know where they'd been placed. An enemy was out there beyond the tree line. I knew better than to chase after her, she might be the enemy. I do, do believe I was an extension of her worst nightmare, crackling branches underfoot, it was fucking Jack, Jack the fucker come again, stalking her. Bright red sparks flew up into a tarry black sky, rained down like sunspots. I dropped to a prone position, readied my rifle, my eye to the sights. There was nothin', nothin' out there but a doe and her fawn chomping on some apples. She'd gone and ripped her jeans, scratched her arms, her face. She hitchhiked home at 3:00 AM, caked with mud, across miles of desert, miles from nowhere, nowhere she felt like she belonged. (pause) This last cup. Truly, I'm so sorry, who I was, what I've done. That metal drip working its way out my brain like a tiny sliver of shrapnel, rust-colored, bleeding out the back of my hand. 30 years plus, and the lump gets smaller, doesn't hurt as much when I bump it. Now it's in my throat. I can speak it. Truly, truly I know the damage I've done. Yeah, we've all been abandoned to the horrors of black glass. We must not be afraid anymore. Might we heal with the first light of day, or will the sun be too hot tomorrow? I anticipate nothing but to tell the truth, feel the wind on my breath, I do believe the past is now! You are who you were, all you'll ever be right now. *No! You are not here!* It's written above the door, but that was last night's dinner conversation. To speak of it will set you free. You fucked up my life Dad, you must tell 'im! Your War cost me my youth, my freedom! Above the line I do believe we can heal each other. I will clear the ashtray. I've got pills to take and know I'm not well. I anticipate a good day in spite of my failings. Have I convinced you yet that she's not dead? Nothing's left undone above the line, there's no beginning or end to the page. No one's forsaken, not even Jesus who once upon a cross believed otherwise. Remember this, she ain't dead! No one ever dies!

And who will I meet on my walk today? I anticipate angels in my path. I'm just a poor scribe who can write through anything, on toilet paper with blood if I must. I know where I've been, drips, tings, the pangs of the heart, and how the wind blows me about, that's the fun of it.

There ain't nothin' worse than a leaking pen in your pocket like your best friend's brains spilling out into your lap. Might as well throw that shirt out. (pause) 7 church bells like what I can't forget. Saw no one on my walk, not even a dog walker. I didn't walk under the sparrow tree, had a fear of being hit with wedding rice. Still I did catch a glob crossing the street, *splat* atop my left shoulder like drool from a camel's eye. You can't ever dodge that shit! Doc was just a hair above the sandbag line, reading a letter from home, dropped him where he sat. I can't sleep in a bunker no more, 130 fuckin' degrees face down in the mud, and play dead. It's stopped raining, these church steps are wet, don't mind it any; my jeans are dirty. A car pulls up, a real live person. "How about them Giants!" Knowing she's a fan.

"Yeah, I love it!" Suzie grins in her Shockey jersey like a proud momma bear.

The meeting hasn't started, but Mike gets up and leaves, doesn't agree on what page we left off on, and should start up reading again in the Big Book, first printed on fat, bulky paper in 1939 it was coined The Big Book. Big mistake, don't need all them religious connotations. Should have called it the Fat One, or the Chunky Book, but they act like it was holy scripture, as if from the mouth of God, sure it's full of good information but bad prose, outdated, sexist, and needs a rewrite. Sill they refuse to change a word of it like Moses himself had brought it down from the mountain. Don't matter what page we're on, heard it all before, it's the same bad prose.

Ann called, we're gonna take a walk with her dog Sky down by the river, where the tracks and the water and the forest meet. (pause) Ed called, he cut the grass for the first time in two years, got some fruit, vegetables, and a juicer.

(again) I'm screaming inside like a landslide, like an avalanche runs from itself. Sky swam halfway across the river to get a stick, as far as I could throw it, over and again like buttoning and unbuttoning a shirt. It was all too much for me, he's a young border collie and I couldn't keep up, had to sit and take my rest. Brilliantly colored dying trees, a sailboat crossing over, a tugboat pulling a barge upstream. Yeah, I need to outsource this pain, collect myself, find a dream, but I fall like a dead leaf to the ground. This cancer's a broken song, a sad song.

I don't want to see her again. Don't want to have her be dead all over again. Two butts in the ashtray. Such a perfect day, but I feel I don't belong here. (pause) Tried Shay, no answer. I did help someone this morning, helped her feel better about herself, such a smart, lovely person. So why all this self-loathing? It's only my body that's failing, and all these limitations will eventually fall away. Again the sun's going out, crowding me out, and ghosts will appear. Above the line we are all childlike, children of God, but the childish beat rocks with sticks and hurt people. I feel sorry for Mike, his pulpit's a barstool. He pushes everyone away and goes home alone. We all only need, and want to be held.

(a walk) And the light stopped me dead in my tracks, pierced the leaves of the tree, orange and yellow and golden like a spear to my heart; I basked for a moment in the full splendor of dying. "God, I am the fruit of thy labor."

*   *   *

I've met a few angels that I didn't know they were angels until after they left. Like the Jewish girl with blue eyes who taught me how to ask. I've made it this far without a fix, but I'm pale, coughing up black stuff. My mind's in the glass, a room outside this one. Yeah, I need another cup. She'll be here tomorrow if I don't jump off today. I anticipate nothing. (pause) Can't catch my breath like you can't box the wind. Did make a few bad phone calls, but they didn't come true. Did a meeting last night, reached out to Mike, talked of my own self-hatred, how I drive others away and feel so empty, alone inside. "If I don't like me, how can I expect you to even care? We deserve better." Sunday morning, a loveseat in shadows, cats, cats, cats, back and forth, running track. I'm grateful I'm not hung over. No, I haven't filled the page yet. I'm waiting on the birds. (pause) Took my 6 pills as prescribed, two shots of air, something for the pain. This cough is bad. I just can't get that feeling like water from a rock, when the word hits the page like an uncaged tiger. And fearlessly what symmetry bowed low in service to the wind.

Sundays are days of nostalgia, too much memory and overwhelming loss. Just get me off this page, onto something new. (pause) Called Ed, like me he's up at this hour, we help each other feel good about ourselves. Yes, we've all been beaten down, rockets, belts, fists and chains, landmines. "From hell, life ain't fair." (pause) Maggie called, they're gonna start up the radiation and chemo come Wednesday, I'll be moving into the hospital with my computer. I don't anticipate being cured, but it'll buy me some time. It's all good, I think. I'd like to make a joke, but I can't. Church bells and barstools, won't wear a crown of thorns or drive nails into glass counter tops. Words come on their own if I leave myself alone. It's not how many pages, or at what cost. I believe in a living, practical God, one who fixes your car, spruces your lawn, one who surgically removes cancer. Me, I'm just a scribe. We all possess such gifts, wonders to perform. If you labor in love, they will love what you do. I love a sushi plate, a manicured baseball diamond, a well-decorated department store window. Jess makes the most beautiful jewelry, it dangles so gracefully, holds a delicate balance of flesh, stone, and wire, twinkles and shimmers in the light. Art must inspire Art as Life should Life itself. I am living Art.

Vanity gives nothing back but broken glass. These gifts are for giving like wind fills the sails of a tall sail ship, words like music still the noise and encourage the soul. When I die I will have been a good scribe. (pause) I've got one last cup to come around. My desk is strong and made of oak. Ed will be a therapist; his hands will cup the water. I know his father like I know my War, we share our trauma. I love Ed. We need all the help there is, we are all practitioners. Above the line God is alive! I'll just eat a good breakfast, make the bed, rinse my cup, and live forever. I anticipate all things to come. Jess will be here soon.

(later) The light arcs from the west through the blinds, I make angels and rabbits and birds on a blank TV screen. I get up too fast and all the blood rushes to my head, makes me dizzy like a walk on the Moon. No phone calls, no mail on Sundays. Something of a nap, but not really a dream. That itch in my throat kept me awake. (pause) Shay doesn't answer. Took a pill that might help me stop smoking, but it only gave me a stomachache. I pray Shay's sleeping upon jet skies, bluescapes with track legs, making diamond flips over jeweled mountains. (pause) Cate says, the preacher said, "God is illiterate." So all those fish in your fishbowl only think they pray, and God hears them. 3 flakes and you're fuckin' out of here! I've got nothing for this cough. Could do some laundry. I need something to read with a heartbeat, need to reinvent myself.

*   *   *

Don't know who won the game, it doesn't matter much, it's just a game, tomorrow's another game. And there's always another page. She'll be here today, there's nothing left to anticipate. Don't remember any dreams, but there are 9 players, 3 stages before any spiritual convergence. (pause) My nephew Danny called, he'll be home for Christmas than back to Iraq for a second tour. I'd like to do somethin', break his legs, send him to Canada, somethin' to stop it. Didn't even come close yesterday to making a bad phone call. (pause) Another cup. Yeah, I have those nightmares, they're sending me back there, "But I've already served, Sir, I've got metal in my leg." Still, I can't seem to stop 'em, end up face down in the mud being shot at. 3 butts in the ashtray. Good days are adding up. (pause) All I know about Jess anymore is her laugh, all that seems familiar. How will she look, will she still have that arch in her foot, a high booty like a rolling hillside, that spunk in her step bouncing her up off the pavement like a glorious high-rise, or will she waddle like an old woman and hog up the sidewalk? (pause) It don't matter any, it's her laugh she's kept, that ebbs and flows and sails tall ships. Look at me, I'm no Willie Moore anymore, can't puff the head off a dandelion. No silver maples, balsams, just sky. Seems we've all grown up. There'll be no pining away, no log cabin, no trip flares. There's that train whistle off in the distance, down by the river. No, I can't hop no freights no more.

Jess is dead, only dead, she'll be here soon. I do believe the dead rise again. She'll take this sackcloth from my eyes and like Lazarus I'll be unafraid to laugh. I anticipate nothing but this moment of truth. I'm outside the black glass looking in. I'll make the bed, brush my teeth. I anticipate angels on my walk. It's me like Odysseus, skipping words like bootprints across the page and forehead. People say, "You look better alive than dead." (pause) I was followed by blackbirds, felt like I was walking in Arles in the fields of Van Gogh. 7 bells beneath the sparrow tree. The Lean Gray Woman with her husky dog comes prancing forward. Crossing the street, we wave like always. The News Man en route, he's too far off for words and determined in his stride. The coffee makers arrive, two new women, "Good morning." We're here for the same reasons. I follow the flight of a mocking bird from rooftop to treetop, and back to Earth.

The News Man returns, gestures toward the sky, "Nice one." The Big Man pulls up, labors up the walk. He's changed for the better, I'm polite. (later) Not even a nap. Jess is 3 hours from here. Got this metal taste in my mouth. Might just have a seizure, kick some walls, start frothing, lick the ink from the page, stick this pen in my eye, swallow my tongue, and take a bite out of my left arm. Ed took all the beatings meant for his younger brother, stood between him and his father. There goes my vision soft on the sides. Above the line there's nothin' love won't do. Lightin' sparks, pink and orange skyscapes like envelopes being opened and nothing inside. Can't see the page, its one black line. No more words.

Leaves fall from the sky like snowbirds. I sit at the bus stop where no bus stops. It's too damn hot! Still, most of you don't believe it. "I won't live another 80 years," says the guy in the smoke shop.

"What about your children?"

"They can fend for themselves."

"But can they melt!" He laughs; I lose on a scratch off. (pause) She's here, checked in, she'll call before she knocks. Best put my teeth in, put on some pants. God, my stomach hurts, can't rid myself of this metal mouth.

*   *   *

Chapter 6

the visit

He has made everything appropriate in its time. He has also
set eternity in their heart, yet so that man will not find out
the work which God has done from the beginning even to
the end. Eccl. 3:11

*   *   *

Maybe these 3 women I'm making don't belong together. What has it to do
with vanity? Still, I don't want them fitted in a row like ducks at a shooting
gallery. This is a strong cup to swallow. Almost a headache. I'm wishing it
were over. It might be raining, it's too dark to tell, don't hear no drainpipe
drip. It's not the refrigerator running; it's coming from behind the glass.
Her hair is white like snow, pure like grace, still long and beautiful. Seems
all I know for certain is her laugh, can't see the way she thinks, not yet.
Don't know her habits these days, just what hasn't changed. In my dream
Jess was singing the most beautiful song. We audience sat on barstools
among the players, you had to keep moving your seat to make room, the
staging area kept changing like one's point of view. The song was a torch
ballad about coal mining, about Harlan. "Black lung, black lung, your
hands I feel cold, as you reach for my heart, torture my soul." It made me

sad. A young blue-eyed boy appeared on a film screen like a home movie against a backdrop of neon beer signs. He was crippled, a nurse was trying to help him walk, braces and all, both his hands gripped tightly along wood railings, and slowly he made forward progress. I knew the boy as a kid, loved him, we were friends, he'd long since died. But not before I'd hacksawed the braces from his legs, fixed the spokes of his wheelchair to his shoulders like Magpie wings. The song Jess was singing fit serendipitously into every movement of the boy. "Down in that hole, down in that cave, I spent my life's blood, diggin' my own grave." And it was as if he flew away! Down gutters and drainpipes, over rooftops and oceans of black heavenly sky, into the moon's red charm. It all culminated in a flood of tearful joy, and standing applause.

Jess's niece Faith, the 16-year-old bleached-blonde is using my last book for a book report; she's making 10 collages inspired by the book. Truly a Blue Choir Girl of Candor, bleached-blonde, I like it. It don't get any better than this, my feet are leaving Earth.

I'm not writing you this; it's just what's been given me to tell. (pause) Took my pills, need a shot of air. Had a message from the Bag Man last night, had little or no desire to call him back. Went to bed. (pause) We had a nice dinner; she the grilled salmon, me the mixed grill. Went to the café, she heard me read a few pages from the last book, didn't read any of this. It was all about running, keep moving, hitching cross-country, "And here it holds no contemplative realm." I'm not sure I'm enjoying this visiting with the dead, but I know the way like a blind man's dog. Took a walk around town, showed her all the shops, restaurants, walked a cobblestone path that reminded me of Harold's milk wagon. Her ass still looks good, she didn't waddle any or hog up the sidewalk. (pause) Blackbirds circle outside my door, but leave me as I walk off. All the color has been taken from sight, subdued by the soft lens of morning's first light. A dew like sediment of grace settles at my feet, I kick it up in stride like a windy sail. A crystal glass blue bird refracts the song from a window's ledge, waves a spectrum of blue ocean graciously overhead. The tree sparrows follow me down the walk, fly past the Inn where she's staying. We turn the page like a street corner. She mentions Rockwell, but it's more like Hopper. That was last night. It really cuts me up, these old pictures, the black and white stuff, but it's here on this page I'm writing. It's snowing. (pause) My clothes are in the dryer. I'm leaving tomorrow for the cure. It's all too real for me now, feel like this cancer is winning the War. They're gonna radiate me Mom, I'll wear an orange halo. They're gonna make me hotter than the sun's ever been. I won't be coming home. (pause) Some people here really like me; why won't I let them? Mary's right in my face, told everyone what I should be doing, "See an old boyfriend!" She puts her lips together and makes a fart noise. I don't care what she thinks, no one here believes her. I won't change my phone number, anyway I've memorized his. You here, you're all a part of my sickness. (later) A dreamless encounter. The wind gusts, the Blue Choir Boy sings, "How do you keep alive?" The song ends. (pause) Another cup. I'm only visiting with the dead. Don't know yet what she wants, how she's stuck, how and if I can help her. (pause) Made a few phone calls. Stayed calm, soft, got sympathy from a bill collector; he'll call me come New Year. Nothing works if you don't work with it. It's too hot for a shirt. Are there too many holes in this story? Need a shower, something to eat. I've got a pile of dirty clothes. I'd like to jump, but I'm afraid of heights. Holes, where bullets pierced the flesh and buttons used to be. Again the music stops. (again) Me and Jess we took a ride, up and down the hill. Just wanna get off, out from the past. Feel like I've been hit by a truck while being nailed to these tracks like a dead fish washed ashore, spread eagle across the page. Where's my tall sail ship? That desperate look in her eyes, I can't help her. I'm only failing at this game of life.

This is all I do is write, all I want to do, all else is vanity. Nothing else matters much, even this doesn't matter. She's dead already, this is all there is to be done about it. Nothing but holes. Again the afternoon is sinking, light from day. I stare off out the window where she once lived. I need to ask her to leave, please, leave me. Storm clouds, but no tears. No lace curtains, just a vacant window, empty space. Do I drink another cup? No, nothing good it seems that doesn't come undone, or knot itself up. (pause) This cup ain't working. I've got these lumps in my throat like I don't know what to say next. What is it she wants to tell me? The air is thick like a jungle path, the wind has stopped, all the world is still. Just to get off this page, but I don't know that I can. If! If I want to. Can't ask her to leave, can't extinguish 30 years with a prayer that the dead might die again. Two sips left, 3 butts in the ashtray. Should give her a call. What is it you want? How do you come unstuck? How can I help you? Help me turn the page. It's 6 o'clock, *Ode to Joy*. Quasimodo puts out the burning lamps, sets the nightingale free. No, I haven't got a clue how to do this; I'm coughing up rainbows in the dry dust, tryin' to make an oasis happen. Yeah, we're all poor, love starved, forlorn. (pause) Called my mom, her last 4 teeth are breaking off. (pause) Shay Full of Grace didn't answer. She's in the dayroom listening as the old woman passionately screams obscenities at her poor rag doll. The music stops, the screen goes blank.

Could do a meeting or feed my jones. Who to call? Which one? No exit. Is this all a joke God and the Devil are playing me for? This cough resonates like a fist in my pocket, a trashy dime-store novel, there's no time for anything and eternity's missing. The glass is black. (pause) She called, I'm tired. Don't know the workings of a clock, if I'll be here come morning. Just to fill the page like this haircut, so it don't have so far to fall out. It doesn't matter any, like the shirt she gave me I left in the back seat of her car, I won't wear it. No, won't wear any advertisements, especially that latex print, can't even wear it inside out. Wouldn't dare regift it. I'm grateful to be alone. Yeah, I'm being eaten from the inside out, can't burden anyone with that. I've got a handbasket full of buttons, bullets and no shirt.

Above the line they got the best pretzels, salted with Dead Sea salt. The ghosts in the glass are too old to barter any like canned soup, used car dealers, and rent-a-cops. I won't call the Bag Man again. I can't be waiting on anyone. I can't see nothin' beyond the black glass like one needs teeth to eat an apple. I like 'em green. That was so good, there'll never be another like it. Can't chase a chicken out of the fryer and back to the chicken coop. This box is made of sand and burlap, oil barrels filled to the brim like dunes on a deserted beach. I'm a headache above the line, listening to Bob Dylan do Mother Goose, and Little Miss Muffet watches a scary movie, eating chocolate donuts with her pants off. "Oh, a big black hairy spider!" I only want to leave you here tied to this chair, drive off in a fast car, forget you all like Shay Full of Grace forgets. Leave you like a memory, a black hole, a workbench lamp still burning in the next room. (pause) Ice cream without teeth tastes so, good, it soothes my throat, makes these lumps like ski slopes. Now the ice cream, it's too cold, and what's hot like coffee's too hot anymore.

*   *   *

The black glass is crying, beads up with black tears, leaves spots on the wall. How will I walk to the meeting without getting wet? Just to connect the dots, put these pages to type; make pictures out from the metal beats, pictures where there were none. It's getting better, we agree, falling into place, good stuff. (pause) Another cup. Still, this drag strip in my throat. Not before long and Jess goes back to Santa Cruz. It's been a good visit, what else is good, she's thinking of moving here, back East. There's a vacant storefront on the outskirts of town, she could get it cheap, 600 square feet, she'd open up shop. She's spoken to a local jeweler in the next town over, there's more than enough business. Jess could work from home, she'd still have her customers, but she's always wanted her own place. There's a good school system here, one of the best soccer teams in the state, plus Maria would live in proximity to Big Charlie, wouldn't have to travel 3,000 miles to visit her dad. Jess would be closer to the Island, her parents. Mildred and

Jack seem healthy, but are aging fast. "They're gonna need me, besides I'm sick of Santa Cruz, been there too long, sun's too damn hot anymore!" Here she'd be only a 100 miles from her brothers, her nieces Faith and Hope.

Jess misses the seasonal changes, the marigolds, the falling of leaves, snow at Christmas, something you don't get out West. Talked with Maria over the phone, she's a sweet kid, a good student, no boyfriends yet, loves soccer. (pause) Again the ashtray is starting over. This last cup has no reason. Told Jess I can't be anyone's lover, I'm a mess, I'd only fuck us both up. This cancer has stripped from me any ideas, illusions about a long-term relationship; still despite my limitations, I'd like to try being intimate without the sex. Just don't want to hurt anyone anymore, not even myself. She thinks we can be good friends, expects nothing, nothing has to change or stay the same. Today she'll talk to Harold; I believe there are some vacancies here. (pause) I'm filling in the holes, or someone's doing it for me. Might be soon I'll have a new neighbor. Feel comfortable with Jess; don't have to be anything other than who I am. I'm not always sure who that is, but I enjoy the company. Really all I've got is this page, there's nothing else alive at this hour. We had a good talk last night; I'm beginning to recognize something other than her laugh, her kindness, fortitude, gentle demeanor. Remember that red cowboy shirt she bought me with pearl like buttons in silver trim. It wasn't my birthday, no special occasion, she just liked the shirt, thought I'd look good in it. I did, it was my favorite shirt of all time. She was like that, always bringing me something, candy bars, pretzels, a new pen. Last night she brought over a box of tea, Throat Coat, to help heal the soreness. Didn't like it much, but now it's all I drink. (pause) The rattle of my desk lamp like trees breaking in the wind. I think the rain has stopped. I should give Ed a call. (pause) Me and Ed, we're good for each other. It's all good. (pause) No walkers, even the sparrows were mostly quiet. Two different moms seeing their kids off to school. The rain hasn't stopped, a persistent steady drizzle keeps me off the church steps. I'm meeting Jess for breakfast after this meeting. I can deal with the chatter, the Big Man holding court in exchange for a dry butt. Arleen asks, "How you doin'?"

"I'm hanging on by the skin of my false teeth." Both she and Marybeth laugh. Brought an apple with me, a book I'm not reading, where I keep this yellow page, jot down these notes. (pause) Stepped out for a quick smoke. Between a walk and a jog The Newsman trots past, in yellow slicker and hat, "Looks ugly today."

"Yeah." (pause)

I don't share the group's enthusiasm. I have to read these promises, but I don't believe them. I eat my green apple. (pause) We're talkin' about God, thought of that goldfish, but I don't speak fish, so what do I know? Nothing about God. I just get these 3 flakes each day, I'm grateful for that. (later) A nap. Two phone messages of no importance. There was a dream but I lost it, can't remember what, my throat scratched me awake. I feel like an ashtray, a coal miner. I should do some laundry. I need a phone call like a dead man needs his rest. Maybe the Bag Man's home from work today on account of the rain. The pages have stopped numbering themselves. We're timeless, and the music stops. (pause) My clothes are in the wash. I can't pretend to be anything different, can't find what it was to feel good about. It's just a blurb, a footnote, these bits, parts. What was that dream? Had breakfast with Jess, a few laughs, got coffee beans, hit the supermarket. It was all good, but she left me with that desperate look in her eyes. What is it she wants to tell me? Tonight we're going Japanese. (pause) Are there no lamb chops? Should cut my nails, they're only getting in the way. Should move to Europe, the Swiss Alps, a blue house, Southeast Asia, live in the jungle, shoot dope, buy me a housekeeper. (pause) Ate some lunch, the last of the orange jelly. Don't feel like listening to anybody. My clothes are in the dryer.

The World Series starts tonight, think the World is gonna loose. My team's not in it. Fires are still burning in California, 500,000 more evacuated from their homes. If it ain't a fire, the bank's gonna take away your house. It ain't a car, but car insurance I can't afford. The price of gas. I'm disgusted by the look of things, the greed between the lines, the small print, the state of health care, that War! The next beach head will be New York City, it'll all go orange in a flash, and the Earth will split, swallow you up, and spit you out like camel drool through the eye of a needle. (pause) Yeah, I've got clean sheets, a desert in my throat and a head full of jones. How many more pages? Like Lazarus come back from the dead, ain't got a fuckin' clue how to live, can't hold on to anything for fear of loosing more. That word is gone, lost, this one like eternity in a handbasket. Who can I call? The Man or the Boss? Can't watch the news, don't need any weather report to know how hot it is. Above the line are only cool things, solar-powered windmills and sun cells on a blue roof, cobblestone, and horse-drawn milk wagons. Even the rocks sing out. Jesus no longer dies for our sins. (pause) Dinner at 6, she's making arguments at me; don't know what it is she needs. I'm not her writer in shining armor, no white horse, I'm just a scribe. Jess got that apartment, 100 yards off to my right, she'll be moving in before Christmas. That one, the one I can't stop looking at, it's all vacant now, curtain-less. Still, I don't know what it is; think she likes me too much. This cup is empty. Again to make the bed, rinse the coffee pot, clear the ashtray, dishes from the sink. All I know is this page, don't know why, who she died for, or how many times I've died. Is eternity bliss? Vanity unfurled like wind on water, water, water everywhere. Are there only potholes? No cumulative lakes? No reservoirs? One blue branch holding back a rock. No blood in the sand, no fingers winding clocks, no 6 o'clock *Ode to Joy*. Please, get me off this page on time, before it all goes orange. I'm not really here, I'm in this hospital sick with cancer. Can't smoke while I write, slows me down some. Dan took me out for a ride, got me out from being a patient. Met Harold in the smoke room, he drives a go-cart not a milk wagon; he's got what Shay's got. Been here 4 days, had only one treatment and the glow machine broke down. Can't go home my computer's here, had I known I'd have gotten a lap top. I'm sicker than most, but Clayton's only 23, he's got an inoperable brain tumor. Rene like Harold like Shay, they'll never leave alive. No, I'm not really here, what's too sad to comprehend. (pause) The bed's made. The light's going out. Can't share my resting place with anyone. Again to brush my teeth. Killed a bee and a fly today just because they didn't fly off. There's no resting place here, fly or die! I need me some wings. Where are my angels? All men are babies, want a tit to suck on and to have their dicks sucked. I don't want to feel anything, up or down, but go sideways out the window, across the line on a cruise ship with a balcony view. It's in the water, all my words. I just might drink them all up, all that's left. Yeah, I'm feeling inappropriate, heartless, hope the Man don't find me here begging out eternity. Again the music stops.

*   *   *

I'm up too early like it's still the night before; don't know who won the game. Black glass. This cup. Didn't trade it all in for a shot. She told me all of what her father did to her. How at the age of 9 he got her drunk, stuck his dick in her mouth. "This isn't easy to say, won't be easy to hear." (pause) Another cup. Feeling sick to my stomach. She said more, "Night after night he came into my bedroom; he'd wake me up, he'd be touching me all over." Like rockets, I thought, he had her pinned to the floorboards, sucking up mud, afraid for her life.

If she didn't do what he said, he'd tug at her hair, "Faster, harder!" He'd pinch at her budding nipples. She'd be made to stick her finger up his ass. "Yeah! Yeah! Oh, yeah!"

"He always felt bad afterwards, guilty I think." (pause) We'd both been raped, countless times, over and again, night after night. No, nothing's awake at this hour, nothing moves. Only black glass, the memory racing like a freight train, pounding out pictures, images of dead soldiers piled in a heap, her on her back, helpless. "I'd leave the light on, but there was no lock on my bedroom door." She was made to promise not to tell or else, she didn't know what, but she feared the worst. She'd seen his temper, seen him smack her mom. "He'd say nice things, how much he loved me, more than my brothers, how he'd protect me from the outside world, keep me safe. It didn't feel good," she was crying, "It hurt." She felt sick to her stomach. "He told me how beautiful I was, my hair, my skin so soft, white, pure, my perfect tiny breasts." She wanted to believe him, felt dizzy from the alcohol, "I was afraid he wouldn't love me." She'd pretend to fall asleep, he'd leave. She'd pray he wouldn't return, wouldn't come back, "I guess God wasn't listening."

It was hard to say anything, but she only needed me to listen, for someone to hear her. We both had a chill. She got up from the couch, turned on the fireplace. This is the oldest inn in the United States, this room, it's petrified, stuck in a different era yet trying to be somewhere else, hence the gas fireplace, both rustic and tacky, looks as if no one's stayed here in years but for these ghosts. A century-old photograph of the old mill down by the river hung above the fireplace, some artificial green and white flowers in an Easter basket on the mantle, another bouquet she couldn't stand that she'd stuffed in a corner behind a bookcase. She had to pull it out and show me. "Yeah, it's fucking ugly." Jess said, Jack had read my book, really liked it, but that didn't make me hate him any less. "No aesthetic sensibilities in whoever designed this place." I held up an Easter basket, "You make this?"

"Fuck you!" She shot into the bedroom and quickly returned holding a black leather-bound portfolio, a smaller photo album. Took her seat back next to me on the couch. Jess showed me all the pictures of Maria growing up. A beautiful girl who wore a perfect smile. Snow white ivory skin, long red curls like her mom, them big green eyes. (pause) Another cup. Again the ashtray is starting over. The black glass is full of ghosts. I'd like to shatter the glass, kill Jack! All the horror's there abandoned on them tracks, tied to them rails, that train whistle down by the river, beyond the glass. You can only hear it in these early hours before dawn, before the War, before Daddy ever came home from work. Rockets and mortars, "Fe, fi, fo, fum!" Closer, overhead then passing, back and forth, over, over and again like giants walking giant steps. He stands at the foot of her comforter. Worse than being hit by rockets or trains is their whistle and pulsing bark, the projected fear of being abandoned, it's greater than abandonment itself. Who is it? Don't ask! But the order of things is lost; there are no page numbers here. There's no one I can call for help, they've taken my voice. Again she felt so alone, helpless. If! And if one hits the roof, you're dead meat! If she were to tell anyone no one would believe her. She'd be made to apologize, or be punished, pull the covers up over her head, forget about it, pretend to fall asleep. Again, he'd be there in the shadows at her bedside, over and again like a bad dream you can't wake up from, or one that keeps you awake. I keep seeing Rodney in the black glass, his last footstep pressed up against my chest, can't breath, tightening its grip, this black bag I've crawled myself inside of, and she's been tied up in knots, tied to them tracks, it's fixed to our brains, unable to get free. We wake up screaming! "Rodney will never die!" Jess is eternity, no beginning or end. (pause) You are not here. Don't fool yourself that you're listening. These sounds are indefinable. Again that smell, walking into my tent, the sweat, the semen, the stench, her endless sobbing.

"You brought her here; you get her the fuck out of here!" (pause) She'd cut herself, her arms, her legs, her chest, into a million little fucking pieces. Me, I'm baggin' Rodney again. She'd promise not to tell. Who? Why? Can't stop it. Blame it on the cat if anyone noticed.

There were pictures from back when I knew her, when we were lovers, some 30 years ago. This Jess I seemed to recognize, something greater than a laugh. Them patched-up jeans, that cocky stance, her long red curls falling gracefully down around her waist, them big green eyes pleading sympathy, beckoning out a mystery, "Please kind sir," a promise of intrigue. Now I know why, all the ways I'd loved her. Her eyes caught mine; I brushed her hair back away from her face. (pause) Never noticed the cuts, she'd hide 'em with cloth, creams, bandages, guess I just wasn't looking, bought all them excuses, cat tales. I had a few of my own. Wish we could start all over again like she'd walk into the room for the first time, we'd sit on that hillside, yeah, I'd gladly burn up all the words I've ever written. If! God, how I loved her, the girl in them pictures. Cats running track on the ceiling above. This rusty cough like orange dust driving me out, how long before this convoy arrives? One, one good rocket breaking glass, like Shay Full of Grace, If! If only to forget.

Her black leather portfolio was bound in leather cord; wrapped twice around, once unbound it revealed her best work. Photographs of bracelets, earrings, necklaces, charms, rings for fingers and noses and toes. Hearts of stone cut from onyx, goldstone, and midnight blue sapphire. Hearts of all sizes, some so tiny as a spark, tombed in metal strands, tightly wrapped like barbed wire, fencing masks like these knots of mine, bloody gauze and bullet scarred. We are still, stuck, stiff, idle, frozen like ice, timeless. "Hearts in Bondage," she called it. It was spelled out, pictured there perfectly, jeweled in wire, seamless. Weeping and pining for love.

(pause) This Throat Coat tea tastes like metal drippings, but quiets the itch. I only wanted to steal her book, make it all better somehow, eternally free her spirit. That was my last sip. Again to clear the ashtray. I need a solar implant, a bottom to this page like a well runs dry, and a desert flower blooms. (pause) Called Ed, "I'm more alive on the page," I told 'im, "More than anywhere else." (pause) These church steps are too wet to sit. A flock of starlings blacken an already dark sky, take over the treetops. A noisy, mean, ugly bird. It's all Shakespeare's fault, or the idiot who thought every bird mentioned in his plays should be in Central Park. Those starlings killed some of my baby wrens a few years back, smashed them eggs to the pavement for no damn reason. I got me a new blue bird house with a copper roof, a smaller entrance that won't fit any starlings. I snuff out my cigarette in a stand up, penis-like receptacle, *Smokers Palace*, gotta get me out from the rain. (pause) Too much chatter in this basement, I haven't yet learned these skills. Mike comes over, shakes my hand. "I know some vets, been through some bad shit and they're fine." He squeezes my hand too hard for my liking.

"Well Mike, I'm happy for them." I don't believe most of what people say, especially those who haven't had a taste. "I never knew a fireman who volunteered to get burned." (pause) Everybody's blowin' leaves, drying 'em out, sucking 'em up like elephants with big rubber noses. There ain't no safe place.

(later) A nightmare. I was shooting cops with silver bullets through silver badges into blue suits wearing high boots like SS Gestapo come to LAPD. All on a flat, wide screen. There were naked black slave girls in the Jacuzzi, we played suck the tit, one girl had 3 of 'em. Some sweet young innocent thing took my dick out from the water's edge and into her mouth. She sucked me good, all of it until I came in my sheets. I felt nothin' but guilt, remorse like Little Jack Horner stuck in a corner.

Had breakfast with Jess, my day was already so late I had a cheeseburger. Seemed we couldn't catch our breath from the night before. (later) I took a walk with myself, it's a beautiful fall evening like October should be, enjoyed my own company. In all my comings and goings I can't stop looking up at her window. Occupant deceased, apartment for rent. She left a message, one last supper. The bed's half made, 6 o'clock, *Ode to Joy*. Feel like a page is missing, she's leaving. Guess I'll be sad all over again. Another cigarette. Pound that nail so far down it splinters the wood. Don't know who to call, the Bag Man or the undertaker. You wouldn't believe me, how far back the hammer goes. We built them tracks. These days I do better on the page than in real life, I've got you over the phone, don't worry there are no consequences here, I'm only listening. "I don't know him," said Peter, afraid for his life, 3 times he denied heaven as the cock crowed thrice. If! If he'd only asked, surely he would have found his way out from the fishbowl. And the music stops. I've got orange eyes, just to get me off this page in time. I've lost count of how many pills to take. There are no birds but stuffed, fat cats with elephant tusks. I'd like to shoot me up dead or alive! Which way is out? Don't care much for this breathing stuff. The ashtray is full, and I love that I'm in it.

"Fuck you, Peter!"

(pause) Called Romulus, he doesn't want to be my friend anymore, he thinks we almost had an accident, and blames me. He needs to drive that Porsche like I would, but he never stole one. Wouldn't take him into the jungle. I'd have to shoot 'im. He couldn't state it clear until I pressed 'im. "You're dangerous." I don't believe him. Yeah, I've survived being killed at least 200 times, he's the one who panicked, slammed on the brakes, no other car in sight; sometimes slow is dangerous. (pause) Called twice more, said I was sorry; he just couldn't let it go. "Fuck you, Peter!"

No one calls but an automated voice offering to consolidate my debts, "Fuck yourself!" It's that time of day when everything dies like a train ride home with no home to go to. No blue house. One last supper before she leaves town. (pause) All cleaned up like a Sunday choir boy. I'll wear my blue shirt, try and put on a bright face.

*   *   *

Enough sleep so that I'm feeling grateful. No bad dreams. 28 days clean and the Bag Mans number has been disconnected. I just had to find that out, it makes things a little easier. I wonder if you're reading this and rooting for me. Are we friends here? We had a nice dinner; it was something from out of the past, but we talked of new ideas. Two plates of pasta with clam sauce, no wine bottles, no sushi, no pop-up targets, trip flares, just being kind. Jess's leaving soon, back to Santa Cruz, back to the grave. Can't be fooling myself any longer, she ain't comin' back, but she ain't dead on the page, never will be I guess. (pause) It's how the words do find me here; make something beautiful of my worth. Took my pills, two shots of air, another cup like pissing rainbows in the dry red dust, dry heaves over an ever-expanding toilet. It's all in the black glass. I'm looking back again, the next room, her workbench lamp still burning, beckoning out like a lighthouse lantern across a sea of fear and darkness, resting at the foot of her comforter. We've been beaten back, the broken ones. This gift of damaged goods, hearts in bondage.

My life is on the page, words like landfill. This cigarette tastes like silk, this throat drop an oasis, eternal bliss in this coffee sip. Words fall like dead leaves, make a sea of parking lots. I feel the wind, naked as a tree in winter. I trust the wind as true. I'll give Ed a call. (pause) Ed's a good person. Despite his dad's repeated beatings, Ed cared for his dying father, forgave the man, knowing he'd been tortured by Partisans while crossing the border. Dad didn't know anything, just that his wife was real sick, had to get her to a doctor at any cost. Ed held his dying father in his arms, they cried each other's tears.

(pause) Left a wake-up message for Jess, hope to see her for breakfast before she leaves. Again to make the bed, rinse the coffee pot, you know the rest. I've no time on my hands for killing time, just this cigarette I'm puffing, sucking myself inside out, spewing marigolds in the dry dust. The glass is black like I imagine my lungs are too. (pause) I rip off a yellow page to make notes while walking. Crash! *Beep, beeping*, it's the trash truck backing up, emptying the page. I'm lost without a tall sail ship in a parking lot of dead leaves. (pause) A tractor-trailer flys past, lights up the road like a penny arcade. I'm moving sideways, timeless, the click of my pen like a neon switchblade. If I were a younger man I'd hitch a ride out from under the sparrow tree. Soon these church steps will be too cold for my bony ass. Blackbirds squawking past into puffed pink and gray clouds like one dead soldier belly-up. I'm wearing my running shoes, but can't run these days. The neighbor's white gate creaks open like a rusty cough, out comes my orange Porsche. The Newsman passes, unwavering, hands in pocket, "It's a good fall morning."

"I like it!"

"It's about time."

I extinguish my cigarette in the penis hole.

*   *   *

She's gone! I'm on the last train out. She cried, held me like a spoon in water. One last look in the mirror, but the mirror's painted black. No, I haven't a clue how to love someone. Ed's the only good soldier left alive. (pause) Now it's this page going soft on the sides, a headache without the jackhammer, lighting and chariots afire, and angels dance a two-step over burning coals, blurring words eternally forever.

(later) It's a perfect fall afternoon, the back wood is still. No dreams I remember, just the slap, slapping of tire tread flapping off the highway. It's this glow machine Ma; I'm lost in a mine field of metal locusts. My dreams are like roadkill waiting on Blackbirds, turkey vultures, to clear my flesh from the plate like dead leaves from a parking lot. It's all this War in my head, Jack at her bedside, groping warm places. Her only bad dream is the one she wakes up to. In a slumberous purr, "Daddy, stop."

He pulls her hair away from her face, "Suck me, baby." (pause) "Promise not to tell."

"Yes, Daddy, I promise."

*   *   *

Have a feeling she's crying now, already missing our time together. She'll spend the night at Mom and Dad's, pick up Maria in the morning, Big Charlie will drive them to the airport. They'll fly home to Santa Cruz, away from here. The music stops. (pause) Jess called twice, "I can't go in there crying." She's parked in an old abandoned Safeway parking lot across the tracks, up the street from Jack and Mildred's. "Fuckin seagulls everywhere!"

"From the sky, I guess, it looks like the sea. Must be a dumpster near by."

"It's so ugly here, just so fucking ugly! I can't let them see me like this."

"It's okay, cry it out."

"I just wanna go home, sleep in my own bed."

"Tomorrow you'll be leaving on a tall sail ship; you'll be coming into port."

(pause) Ate a green apple while walking the other side of the street under the old snarled tree. It's a good day for falling through, words like snowbirds on a blank page, and white milk trucks. She's hurting, more than afraid, it's worse than an abscessed tooth. Sure, she has regrets, ifs, don't know how lucky she is, it wasn't me she married. Above the line no one needs a couple. It's a pale sky, no tears, the sun's not so hot when stuck behind a rock. This pen works, when it don't there'll be another. I've stopped numbering pages, but you know it wasn't up to me. This cup is just a cup like a bullet leaves a gun, leaves a hole. Yeah, I've got metal in my bones, her workbench lamp still burning in the glass.

One last cup like snapshot, I know them jeans, them curls, that perfect stance, she's laughing. Again to make the bed. It's that sinking time of day again. I'm flopping like a fish out from the fishbowl. A black cat leaps atop my loveseat, stares me down like her next meal. "See here, the turkey vultures got first dibs." I scare her off by coughing like a Blackbird, "Caw, caw."

She stands where there are no curtains anymore. Yes, she once waved to me, waved me home. I was younger then, I'm older then that now.

*   *   *

Chapter 7

coat of arms

The fool folds his hands and consumes his own flesh.
Eccl. 4:5

*   *   *

It's raining, but not on the other side where fires are burning. I've got no breakfast partner this morning. Pray she had a safe night, sleep without interruption, good dreams. I can't remember any. This cup's too hot. That look in her eye is fixed in my brain. I know why but can't fix it like she can't stop this War in my head. I want to take off this soldier suit; this helmet only hurts anymore. The tap, tapping of a metal drainpipe, bits, scraps, dripping down my pant leg, her hair pulled back, around, over her face. Over, over and again. And all the good soldiers eat themselves up. I'm already smoking my next cigarette, and haven't finished this one. And who can you love when your father has raped you? He's too old, sickly, harmless, kind; he pays for her gas with a credit card and sends her packages of fresh meat. "I won't care when he dies, I want him dead. I won't cry." Still, I believe she will. It's like this cigarette I'm using to light the next one, and another like a chain gang working, shackled, driving home spikes, and she her needlepoint like she's tied to them tracks by a warm wooly scarf.

(pause) It's only me killing myself, all these bullet holes, an empty bottle of Jack, a large, almost-empty bottle of Listerine on the coffee table. I can't be her dad, lord and savior, don't wanna be, she can't find my way home. The ashtray is full. I'm trying not to hate myself. If he only once, and not while having his dick sucked, said she looked pretty, didn't make fun of her nose. There are no tricks to staying alive, but staying alive. Do I walk in the rain, believe my own lies? Are there no bullet holes in every red barn? How many rings circle Uranus? Yeah, he's much too friendly, must be running for office. He only feeds then beats the dog, all his newspapers rolled into clubs. Again, over and again. The middle of the road is being devoured; in turn we will swallow you whole, dividers, barricades, double yellow lines, crime scene tape.

We're crossing over. I've only got scars anymore, no new or used guns in the house, no fresh tracks. This seat belt ticket is a misdemeanor. Mr. State Trooper leans back on his gun and laughs, "Busted!" There's that train whistle again, freeing me up. I've got a letter from my shrink, don't have to wear a seat belt, can't sit in tight places, this anxiety is hazardous to my health, I prefer windshields, bullets, and twisted up metal parts. And the good judge, she sides with me, throws his ticket out.

I'm grateful we didn't have sex; I would have only had to leave. Don't tell the nurse you're sick, he'll just come home from work, find you sleeping. It ain't safe. Seems like there's nowhere to heal, all hands are groping. Isaac was never the same, couldn't just walk out of that movie into the present tense, held onto that seat until it consumed him. That page has been rerouted, disencumbered. We must once again rise from the dead, over and again, having shed all buttons now we must loose our shirts. A choir of angels singing, the metal drip, drippings of our hearts. I'll call Ed; he knows about these things, he's got a hacksaw. (pause)

Can't find a ride, but the rain ain't so hard that I can't walk. I'll wear my boots, ball cap, and waterproof jacket. (pause) Threw a curbside paper up onto a porch. No walkers. I've got a dry step atop these church steps. Some bird lands close, but it's too dark to tell its name. I'd like to speak bird, make new friends. (pause) The red in my left eye is cancer. There's more wind in this room than a hot air balloon. Now Mike's gonna read from the Fat Book, and tell us twice his name's Mike! Wouldn't be here if I absolutely didn't have to be here. All I really wanna do is get loaded. Here comes the Big Man blimped full of gas, toxic, pulpiting jails, tall tales, Wars he never fought, and died for. Intoxicated by a wind of his own making. I take another sip of Throat Coat tea, scribble something else, and swallow my tongue. Home is on the page. (later) It's an all-day rain, bucket after bucket full. That writing workshop's a drain, don't want to stroke or be stroked, could be home writing. That nap only left me tired. Kill the hunchback, kill the bird in the birdcage, kill anything that can't fly. You expect me to sit here and absorb all this landfill, kill and be killed in a suit of armor. Can't swim in the lake, and don't eat the fish. I could never be what Jess wants me to be. Empty soup cans, torn pages, dead lighters, and pens that don't work. Who will remember any of this? Is there no urgency among you? (pause) Another cup. I need a number that connects, a cigarette that never burns out, a shot that stops me! You can't read it off your sleeve, cry when it ain't on the page. You can't nail it down like me in this chair. You still smell marigolds, but you've got metal in your mouth. So what, Mom wasn't there to give you your milk money, maybe she forgot, didn't care. Maybe she was busy sucking Jack off. Tell me why, how you cut yourself, was it a sharp knife, a razor, a rusty nail, a piece of glass? Was it because no one believed you, because there was no one left to tell? Why you kept buttoning and unbuttoning your blouse until all the buttons had been consumed. How you drank your own blood, fearing you'd lost too much already, and didn't really want to die. How the blood caked up in your hair like a Brillo pad. If! If only to cut off all your hair! Why you turned on the shower but didn't move, lay there in a ball of sweat, afraid, motionless, had to listen, always having to listen to them metallic screams between your ears. And the cold, pink, gray tile made you wanna puke. How Aunt Molly's death, your only real mom, left you breathless, weeping, pining, lost. Tell me why you're ill-suited to live in a fishbowl, and I'll show you how a dead man floats. Tell me how much you hate yourself. How ugly you are. And why in God's name would any man rape you? You're pathetic! Tell me how angry you are, how'd you'd like to kill Jack with a pickax in his sleep, hack, hacking away so he'd never wake up. How'd you'd break his ribs apart, pull his heart from his chest with a crowbar, and stomp it into the floorboards in your best Sunday boots. Tell me how good would that make you feel? Would you cry, cry tears of joy, tears of freedom? For once, tell me the truth. Yeah, it came from hell, life ain't fair. Tell me I'm not sick, not failing. Tell me you're not dead, and I'll come back to life.

The ashtray is full like the page is my refuge, out of necessity this is where I live. You say I don't play nice, tell it to your dad, this ain't no misdemeanor, parking ticket. I'm over it! Above the line! My name's not Isaac, Lazarus, or Job, I'm no test monkey, no sacrificial lamb. (pause) The rain's stopped; it's a peek-a-boo sun. Jess called, she and Maria are on their way home. I'm emptied out and safe, but still this desperate need to use myself up. Can't write this noise without pay, paying a price. My throat is shutting down, slamming shut. The slapping of tire tread, a field of metal insects. Mom, I can glow with the best of 'em. (pause) Threw out that old plastic milk jug, into the recyclable-bin. There's nothing left to tell you, haven't another minute to waste.

*   *   *

First line of the day. First cup. Turn up the heat, turn up the music. I'm coughing up dry dust, and the wind chimes. I've got all the windows open trying to air myself out. So where are my angels now? This coffee isn't working, everything hurts. What I need isn't alive. And again I must empty the ashtray, make the bed, put my house in order, and make it so no one knows anyone lives here. (pause) Feel better having eaten something, half alive. The patio is swept; there are no dishes in the sink, no blood smell. Still, I'm sad like a broken treaty. Blue jay squawking, show me another way. Bruises, a few more holes. Don't know who to call, think I'm stuck on this page. Still, I'll pull myself up, ain't finished yet. (pause) Can't keep the dead leaves from filling up the patio. I've got my thumb rock, just ask. And the page turns. (pause) Again Shay Full of Grace don't answer, maybe she's sleeping or lost the phone somewhere between the sheets and the bed pan. I'm tired of beating the world back with a stick. Last cup, last song. What I need is a haircut. Don't know what I want to hear next. Yeah, I miss my friend. (pause) Are there no angels in hell? I need a shot of life like a bike ride, a jog in the park, a parachute jump. Two, two butts in the ashtray, and I can't catch my breath. Something must matter, is there no life beyond the page? I'm only missing me like a sad song makes you cry.

(later) Made a few phone calls but nobody's home. How many more bullet holes atop bullet holes before I break through to China? Should take a walk into town, need cigarettes, cough drops. Need something to eat, something other than my left arm. I've got a barking dog in my throat, rabid, unchained.

*   *   *

Up and down all night. Still yawning. (pause) Some cold water on my face. Still orange. Can't sit up straight. I'm feeling guilty about everything. I'm consuming myself into billows of smoke like a refinery pumps black soot and oil fields burn. That yellow smut was once was a blue sky. My muddy boots, metallic wings, and filthy sackcloth, I left them at the door. We're looking back at ourselves in the dirty black window glass. All my clocks tell different times. This cough resonates, echoes of an empty drum, the price keeps going up. I'm burning up. (pause) I need a new pair of glasses.

Jess called last night from Santa Cruz, she and Maria got home safe. Maria liked visiting with her dad, two months and they'll be moving back East. Not really, she's dead, been dead, all this happened some time ago. Still, I can't take my eyes off her window; pull myself out from the black glass. (pause) Again the ashtray is starting over. One last cup. It's all true; I just don't know what time it really is. The wind is silent, nothing moving. It's too dark for birds. I've got no one to talk with but this page. Above the line it don't matter any, no one needs anyone here, not even oneself. Words seem to come on their own like holiday cheer, "We wish you a merry Christmas," out of nowhere, an anonymous tip. I must nurture the wind, stand outside the glass, empty myself and wait. I do believe in wind and grace, and not all works of men are of good intent, but only those from the hand of God. A fan blows hot air but can't uproot a tree. An air conditioner keeps you cool but can't move your spirit. My cigarette blows only smoke. Wind and grace can do all things, quake the Earth, divide the sea, and knock you off your horse. We now have bombs that can do all that, but kill all things. (pause) Above the line there are no bombs, no self-annihilation. No nuke will take you out to lunch. You must hear what can't be heard. Above the line we are all scribes. Grace is a hat trick. This last cup never runs out. Two, two butts in the ashtray, this one I'm smoking. No, I haven't any excuse; my guilt is a useless commodity. God must have brought me here, where the page has no lines and the wind blows from left to right like a picture book, flopping scenes in and out of a fishbowl. Above the line the Red Sea parts without a stick, don't even have to ask. (pause) That cough sent me reeling. It's a drag being human. Extinguished my cigarette, took my last sip. One giant yawn, but there's no beanstalk to climb, no blue house made of gingerbread, no bucket for Jack or Jill to fill, no page counts. It's in the doing I am revealed, making small words on a blank page. I will rinse the coffee pot, clear the ashtray, make the bed, powder rocks to slag. I'm not really eating myself, only dying in turn. There's that train whistle again, tracks like bullet holes, and pulsing bark, down by the river where no fish fly. Again to take my pills, straighten that picture on the living room wall. (pause) Ed didn't answer, no room left on his voice mail. Pray he didn't shoot himself in the foot, go stiff on the window ledge like a postcard. (pause) Could see my own breath while walking, my own mortality. No sparrows in the sparrow tree, last night's rain has washed away all wedding rice. It's a killing frost upon the leaves and grass like a sad song's refrain makes my eyes fill and tear. "I am King here, tied to this heart by the King's chain." It glistens on the painted-up laugh of a pumpkin face, scowls from car windshields that must be scraped. Words break apart. (later) Not really a nap, half awake, knew I was dreaming. Saw Jess walking toward me, backlit, she moved with the light like leaves in the sun, her feet above the ground as if floating. She wore a leopards coat and a scarf of lamb's wool. She smiled a whole smile like a perfect autumn day.

*   *   *

The Big Man cornered me on the church steps, "You could have talked to me privately, and didn't have to say it to the group."

"I was upset at the group. I didn't mention any names."

"You made it sound like it was my fault Jessica died."

"I never said that, you misunderstood me."

He tugged at his pant belt, "I've been talkin' about it with my sponsor."

"Good." Knowing he'd never go, didn't believe in it, but said it anyway. "You need a therapist."

"I'm just trying to make amends." He did a two-step, took his arms from his hips and folded 'em over his belly. I didn't wanna engage if he wasn't gonna get real. "It was just a ploy!"

"A ploy for what?" He couldn't answer that, acted like he'd never spanked anyone. "I've made my share of mistakes." I walked off because, because I needed to walk away. And the music stops. (a long pause) Made them doctor appointments, eyes and mental health. It's that time of day when everything sinks like I only want to hurt myself, make glue of a dead horse. Two butts in the ashtray. I'm losing my voice but not the words. You know everything I do. Flip the page. Above the line is a smoking gun, *burp*, all the religion I need, God's like wind on a page, I've nothing to pray for. (pause) Jess's mom called, she's feeling bad, guilty, remorseful, banging her head against a wall of transparencies, a wind of her own making. She blames no one but God. Yeah, she blames herself, what she should have done different but couldn't, until death do us part. She's cooking him dinner, pot roast, his favorite, doing his laundry, sleeps in his bed. She misses her little girl, her best friend; she's no one to talk with. Me, I just listen. She cries bitter tears, consuming herself from the inside out, "I'm sorry."

"It's okay to cry, don't apologize."

"God bless you." *Who* I thought, *your God or mine?* (pause) This Throat Coat tea just makes me smoke more, I'd shoot myself, but it ain't me to blame. I won't fold the page and stuff it in my pocket. That blue house on the window ledge is a lie; I'm moving in, I'll overturn a few tables. No, I haven't seen a blue or red bird all day. (pause) The bed's made, the ashtray cleared, my lungs are black. "What's your pain level? 1 through 10."

"7."

"That's upsetting; we want you to do better."

"Make it a 5."

"We can't do that."

"I can write through the pain. (pause) I've stopped counting pages."

Why can't she ask me how I feel? She's never heard of Henry Miller. (Pause) I never liked pot roast. Yeah, I'd like to leave the last line blank, but not yet. Didn't kill a fruit fly because it flew away. Above the line everything flies.

*   *   *

A good night's sleep, feeling well rested. Heard rain through the night, it was comforting somehow. I'm somewhere between the metal drips, dream and song like black glass looking in. Two butts looking out from the ashtray. Footsteps on the ceiling, the heat is clanking up like a slow train comin'. Don't know where I'm going, what happens next. I think it's Tuesday, know it is, but don't want to know. Is there no way to rid myself of numbers? Cats running track like a fish feeding frenzy, must be that time. Time for pills, need a shot of air. (pause) The black glass is sectioned off in squares, inlaid white stripes, what's acceptable and not like chapters, movie scenes. I need a view, a reason to be on this page. Hey Mildred, when, where, how do you draw that line? The ashtray is full, I feel like I'm missing. That's me in the black glass, the ghostly truth. I don't owe 1,000 bucks to the Bag Man. I should give Ed a call, see if he's still alive. (pause) That feeling, something's askew, knew it without calling. Ed doesn't answer. I need to fly, fly or be crushed. He might be better off dead like all us good soldiers, those who died tryin' to be good. Above the line there are no lost souls. Here I yearn for recognition like Dick, Jane, Spot, and Vincent, see Spot run, but it's never far enough. Dr. Gachet was blown away by my last book, it don't matter any, it's this page I'm on. Jess thinks the book will hit, splat up against the outer wall. Now you see me, see, it's this book I'm writing. Maggie the radiation-oncology nurse really gives a damn, loves her job, helping people, got me my own room, something to gargle with that soothes the burn. I don't want my name on that wall, won't consume myself in one last shot. Yeah, it's a tragic mess; the world is wrong side up. I'm just a scribe tryin' to stay right-sized. I've already died too many times; I'm like Lazarus unbound, invincible to myself. Got this page in front of me, a word on my tongue, fire closing down my throat. There's nothing to fear, death must have its moment of truth, its day in the sun. Life's but a powder flash, eternity a bullet ride. Clear the ashtray, make the bed, I've got these 6 last teeth and one essential book I'm reading. What's left of God in this world? What is it that Mildred and the Big Man don't get?

The wind blows dead orange leaves about, circling my boot heels. It's a cold church step where I sit. I retrace my words, where am I missing? My nose's running, I'm blowing out smoke, discounting my breath. This is my yellow sheet I take on the road, not the one I had to write a 1,000 times for Mr. Horner, *I will not talk in class.* (pause) The Newsman waves back, we say nothing, nothing about the weather. Man's an endangered species, too many pesticides. Mom's been milked out, bees don't come home anymore. The sun's goddamn angry! It's a sea of dry spit, that allusive blue house, I'm sinking straight through to China, If! If only to buy the farm. I've got this metal taste in my mouth. God's been aborted, the Big Man spins another fable like the tooth fairy come down from the cross. There's a moment of quiet beyond the black glass, God's here, under my tongue, that's where the cancer's at. I shoot out after the meeting, not wanting to talk with anyone. (later) No dreams, no phone calls, no real mail. Don't really want to be awake. Where's Ed? The sun's too bright, hurts my eyes. All these pages won't bring Jess back. I'm alone here with my cough, can't get the metal out. These words won't change what Mike says, over, over and again, won't shorten my life any, this cigarette will surely work. I don't believe you! God is Art.

Who to call? Don't really want to make the bed, take a walk, sit on the porch. Would like to drive a fast car into the Great Wall of Mirrors. Don't know why, just, just because it hurts. The ashtray is full of ashes, hot coals, and bone chips. I will go the way of all the good soldiers, none of whom been canonized. No wrens in my blue bird house, no God in your house of God. God don't live in no fancy fish tank. It's just a page you can't number, just, just because no one's going home. It's this here, this page I'm on. (again) Another nap, a series of lost dreams. Maybe it's the coffee that's metallic. One phone call that didn't count. Some leaves are refusing to fall like it's the wrong time of year. I'm only feeling stuck, sunburned, orange leaves wallpaper my throat, coughing, but nothing comes up. He's pouring soup from a can, flips mud cakes on the skittle. The rich eat the poor, and the poor eat themselves. (pause) Got a ride to the store but can't eat pretzels anymore, can't swallow. I'm confused. That allusive blue house Mildred bought into, did she stay there for the kids, did she need his money, or was it love, that she still loved Jack? That white picket fence that the Big Man wears like a crown of thorns. He's never at home; home's a no comfort zone. Eddy, Eddy, come out, come out wherever you are. I love you like we all want to be like Jesus and die for your sins, make them our own. How can we ever stop hurting ourselves? I want to kill your ancestors, torture your dad, and drive your mother out from the house, out from the dream. That sinking feeling that I'm all alone here, but I know better. My throat's screaming like desert heat, a gaping wound. 10 down, 25 treatments to go, I'm losing my voice; soon I'll go silent, dumb like a stone. Keep writing. Yeah, I'm coughing up red wine.

*   *   *

Morning blackness, don't remember any dreams, somethin' bit my ear. Need to splash some water on my face, I'm going orange, can't stay awake. Just how fragile are we? Who's cutting you up? Need to keep my finger out of my ear, the gun from my mouth. No, I don't need a stronger cigarette. Didn't hear from Jess yesterday, she's busy packing up shop. 3 butts in the ashtray. (pause) Another cup. I need to pay the rent, electric, phone bill, not the Bag Man. Tomorrow's pay day, and I'm not already broke. I like the way words look on the page like tall ships at sea, white caps, wind and sails. She's coming east. Need some new PJs, some pullover shirts, long and short sleeve, buttonless. Everything tastes of metal. I'm not looking out on a blue house, took it from the window ledge, and nailed it to the wall. I'm not folding my arms, but putting hand cream on these wounds. Feeling grateful she died first and I get to write this; there's always somebody leaving, somebody left. This time again it's the other guy. Soon, my turn is coming.

Shay Full of Grace has had MS some 25 years now, slow, progressive; it's taken all but her breath away. My throat's a glue patch, pain's up there on the page count. I don't know, maybe 10,212 Christmas's ago I was standing on the front steps of my parents' home sucking down a cigarette. Shay and her husband pulled up, he helped her out of the car. Hadn't seen her in 3 months, couldn't believe how far her disease had progressed. She could hardly even lift her legs to step. He held her up against himself, his arm around her waist. She smiled, "Merry Christmas." Slowly, very slowly they made their way along the railing, down the walk, up the steps. Slowly the tears came, my eyes filled, my voice cracked, "Merry Christmas." I wanted to sing Christmas wishes, "We wish you a merry . . ." but couldn't. Held the door open. (pause) Now these days I can't even get her on the phone. Above the line there are no wheelchairs, diapers, metal bits leaking from my leg, and memory loss counts for nothing. Am I these many pages from home, that final resting place? There's fish in them bullet holes where the black pond meets the black window glass. Grace happens in God's time, in the turning of a page. Again the ashtray is starting over. I've got this one black cup of coffee left. Yeah, it won't make a difference.

Still, I just can't sit here, arms folded and play dead. Don't think I'll call Ed this morning; all these years and I can't seem to find Myles anywhere. An ambulance siren piercing black silence, the taste of blood and metal, *whoop, whoop, whoop*, Rodney's black bag fixed to my lap. God, it never stops, this invincible memory of mine. *Beep, beeping*, another garbage truck backing up. A distant train whistle, Jess is on that train, puts her fingers to her lips and whistles at me because, because I'm cute. (pause)

Made the bed for the first time in two days, opened the blinds. I'm on a slide diet, Jell-O, pudding, yogurt, apple sauce, anything that slides down. Don't want any stomach tube for feeding. Don't count the pages, you might wake up dead. Shay can't add or subtract, I'd like to stuff her like a turkey, make her like a Thanksgiving centerfold, bon apetit. Can't seem to keep my finger out of my ear. (pause) Why is it that black glass at night is sinking fast, and in these early morning hours it's full of grace? I am the truth at this moment. Get me down off that cross you wear around your neck. Why are there no medals of Jesus rising from the dead? Yes, don't ask, you know my name. I'm the good thief.

*   *   *

Chapter 8

windswept

What has been is remote and exceedingly mysterious.
Who can discover it? Eccl. 7:24

*   *   *

This chapter begins on a cold church step; the stone breaking apart, its steeple has toppled. Space for rent, flattened, and made room for a parking lot. The neighbor's gate flies open, my favorite orange Porsche powers out onto the street. Me and the Newsman exchange waves. Like the Old Woman in the shoe, Mildred once believed in white lace, curtains, and carry-on luggage. Soon this step will be hot enough to pop corn. We meet in the basement, but too many get stuck there. Here comes Rebecca with her new perfect baby girl. "How are you?"

"I'm all right."

"Just all right?" She asks.

"All right isn't so bad." She turns the corner. Here comes Uta, we do it again. "Okay."

"Are you really okay?" She looks deep into my eyes, smells of patchouli.

"No, it's your turn. How are you?"

She smiles, "Just like you." She waves her hand like a blessing over her heart, like that old orange Porsche she's in mint condition. "It's a beauty, ain't it?" (later) Not much of a nap, a scratchy throat kept me awake. Still, it was nothin' compared to this. The day before that I was to sick too write, first time ever I'd been stopped, they thought I had pneumonia. There's a wind here now to be made note of, whips the back wood into shape, chimes its own chimes. My entire body aches like I'm living under a boot. No mail, no phone calls, just another page, but I do love this wind. (pause) Jess called, she's at work and feeling good about it. We both love our jobs. She's got Maria, I've got this page. Maria's got a soccer game; I've got one last chapter after this one. (long pause) Ed doesn't answer. It's that sinking time of day. Can't sleep, dead awake. It's a War song I'm playin' while filling up the ashtray. It's hard to get up, and get up, and up again. Called Tom, my new sponsor, but I don't know what I want from him. I'd like to crawl up; still, you can stop me whenever you please. Can't breathe but for this wind. It's all vanity I guess, with nothing left to finish if you're not counting. Give me something that doesn't break like babies being born and holiday cheer. It ain't a postcard offering but one branch of blue sky that keeps me afloat. And the music stops. Still sailing. We get to do it again, the bed, the ashtray, rinse and clear. Most of you don't want to hear it. No, I'm not dead on the page, not feeling good enough to die. It's in the wind that stops you, knocks you off your horse, and the sun will melt your boots like tar on an abandoned, desolate stretch of dead-end highway.

*   *   *

Needed them pain pills first thing. No word from Ed. One pen dies and another takes it's place. Just like this cup of old black Joe. When I'm not looking the right words fall into my lap. I can hear all that the wind moves about, leaves, chimes, barn doors. It's payday, All Souls Day, my dead godmother's birthday. It's her picture of a soft gentle boy laid back on a hillside that hangs off center over my bed. *We popped the heads off dandelions, and grew up by and by.* All you departed souls rise up and sing. This is an offering of peace in memory of all my dead friends and relations. (pause)

Had dreams of my teacher doing his laundry, expressing pure emotion seemed to be the order of the day. Where do the sheep graze? The rent is paid, electric, cable. I need everything from the food store, milk, bread, cheese, pretzels. I like it when the wind talks. Took my pills, two shots of air. There's almost always laundry. I like it when there's no time to kill, when all the words count. These bullet holes are only healing. I like it when the wind chimes one beat. This entire page exists above the line.

I am at one with the black glass, inside and warm. I will empty myself onto the page, make music of noise. I am in the service of thy grace. I will make the bed, greet angels on the side of the road. At this moment I am all of nothing. 7 church bells, a walk among the dead leaves. No one tells the truth anymore, or cares what it is. (pause) These church steps have no bells. Blackbirds squawking darken my view. There are many leaves that still haven't fallen. Light just beginning, a mild enough temperature, a cooling breeze. Its peaceable here, this yellow sheet, a pink and blue sky, red leaves. Forgot my cough drops. The penis eye is smoldering.

"Good morning."

"How are you?"

"Like any other morning," the Newsman replies.

Nothing's the same, I think but don't say it. He gestures behind, two youngsters in tow, "Got a couple grandkids."

"Nice." *See, it's a different morning,* again I don't say it; they trail off into the pavement. Here comes the Big Man; I only want to duck, ascend. Morning repeats itself in glad tidings. I don't believe him. (pause) Can't type two words without making a mistake, it's the morphine. Had a can of supplement paste for lunch, it made cobwebs in my mouth, a cup of applesauce, it's all so tedious, hard enough to swallow. I don't count my days, might even get loaded after this meeting and stop all this nonsense. Don't know if I'm really here, but I do feel like I'm dying. (pause) The speaker, she'd been molested by Uncle Ward. As it goes around the room no one mentions it, no one heard it, like she didn't say it, like it never happened. If we ignore it, it'll go away. "You'll be fine," says Mary, a chorus of bobbing heads. Someone talks of hiding bottles, another pours them down the kitchen sink. Someone's fear of talking, fear of crowds, what to make for dinner? What to wear? Why all this self-loathing? Why all this fear? No one speaks of horror, seems no one remembers Uncle Ward. (pause) Outside I make small talk with a pedophile with one eye on the children waiting for the school bus. I'm confused, when and where to throw stones. (pause) I get a haircut. Have breakfast with myself, avoid sitting with Romulus and the speaker. I read my book, feel sad that we're not friends anymore. He really helped me once, helped me believe in myself.

(later) Sparrows feed on my pretzel crumbs. (pause) Left a message for Nancy, gave her Derk's number, he'll illustrate her children's book. (again) Been to the supermarket, the bank. Got a date and a time for a reading in New Haven. It's a dead afternoon but for these sparrows. I'm feeling abbreviated, that sinking time of day again. This coffee lacks wallop. I'll pay the phone bill, dress up in my father's clothes, eat some raw fish. It's out I want. Again to make the bed. Someone knocking at the door; I don't answer it. This haircut itches; need a shower, a change of shirt. What is it I've run out of? Blue jay squawking. Don't know how to make this next transition, which picture to be in. Might just go ahead and cut myself off. There's too much soup in this pie. And the music stops. I'm feeling dirty and lost, just get me off, off this page on time. I need some real intimacy, reindeer and a sleigh. I'm living from pain pill to pain pill. This is the hardest thing I've ever had to do, be this sick and write. Why dig up them bones? I'm here, beyond belief. I must finish! Above the line, no one is dying.

*   *   *

Don't know how many days I've lost, what time is it? My senses have all been dulled, can't think my way out. Too many holes I'm falling through. Again to put out the trash. Everything hurts, *Caw, caw*; they all want a piece of me. Time is running out, sideways, out my ear. Ed didn't make it, broke apart against the rocks on some distant shore. Jess is dead! I'm a dying fool. (pause) I'll slide down some pudding. So Jess moved back East with Maria, and it was good. What other discoveries need to be made? Can't make me over, fake a happy face. There are no chimes, whistles, or bells. I've got a fist in my throat, these boots can't walk. There's nowhere I'm going to. It's all only dead anymore. Me and the girl, me and Ed. (pause) Put out the trash, an empty milk container, only junk in the mail. Again I'm starting over, what's already over. Having skipped that stone once too often, played soldier too many times. It's all vanity, but for mud and sky. Are there no sins, no sad songs we haven't made our own? Get me off this page, I'm losing ink fast. Got a tall, fresh, lemon-scented kitchen garbage bag. This page is bent like a gypsy. That line just brought me back to life. The back side, facing forward. All my best friends live in soup kitchens. I wear jungle boots and sackcloth, my hair's too short. The page is full, the patio needs a sweep. There are no dishes in the sink. Don't know if I'll ever chew again. Black glass, who is it? A distant train whistles, runs only freight these days. Jess, it's only me missing you, who I once was, who should I believe?

*   *   *

Trying to wake up. Put some order to my house before the thief gets here. I've only got these dirty clothes I'm wearing, no trash, no guns of any type. I need for this coffee to work, need to speed things up; the timeline's all distorted now, distant, but all I've got. I'm here and lost, there is no future.

Jess came and left, came back again, but only stayed a short time. Died, and was born again, forever. Another train whistles. I'm feeling trudged upon like a black and blue weed stuck up between the cracks of pavement. 3 butts in the ashtray. Again the page turns. I'll do the meeting I missed yesterday, eat a few donuts, read from the fat book. I'll take my place on the left facing the door. Nothing behind me, no one gets past my watch. Above the line is void of text; no one has to read this. Jess is home to stay, dead for sure, no, nothing to figure out. The smoke shop opens an hour and a half from here. I'm not killing time, it's killing me. So this is the bottom, no goldfish down here, like my tongue's been put through the shredder, no sign of China. I hit them metal keys with a vengeance; all that's mysterious is how the words punch me out of myself. Where have all the goldfish gone? Turned to raisins, prunes, glue and cobwebs in my mouth. You get 3 minutes to talk, that's it, and then you gotta shut up! God, help my disbelief. What if death ain't all it's cracked up to be, who will torch the wind, will there be no complaint? (pause)

The yellow house I pass on my walk each day has a porch and door lights shaped like large tulip bulbs; they illuminate the small country home in orange fishbowls like a dated postcard. Such a perfect façade. If! If only it were blue. She would have done anything for me, If! If she'd only kept herself alive. (later) I'm coughing up snow-capped mountains, pretending it's not blood. It's an all-day chime, all you get from a hurricane this far inland. It's not a good time to be a polar bear; the Artic is melting. It ain't so remote, so mysterious, soon it will be finished. Just to get this cup of coffee down. Phil's missing a foot, cut his toenail to short. Tim's got a tube in his throat, he and I spit up the most. Rene's strapped to that wheelchair; you gotta put the cigarette to his lips. It's MS, not any cancer that's killing him. All he wants from life is not to die here. Together we are the 4 Horsemen of the smoke lounge. They've increased my morphine, it makes a difference. I've lost 7 pounds in the last week, need more paste. One phone message from Jess, she lives here now where there are no curtains and only the dead speak clearly. The water's rising, south-southwest of the Island. Land cracks and swells like vinyl melts in the sun. Sold two books today, got some new music. There's no safe place, seems all the relatives are waiting on my testimony. I'm sick of being sick, it's too much work. I've got a mouthful of sores. I've got enough morphine in me to sedate a horse, but not the horse in my throat. Tim's getting a transfusion; Rene hasn't been outdoors in over a year; Phil's still missing that foot. Maybe I need to give it up, all this dying, it's time consuming. Rene's been here 4 years now, there's no one he doesn't know, but what they don't know, he stopped depositing empties back when Stewart's took away his milk wagon. Once this book is finished, I think I'm done.

This morphine can't complete a thought. The longer you're here, the bigger the hunchback. What are you holding on for? Life's a trigger pull, eternity a screaming bullet. No blindfold, please. And you take your place among a sea of white crosses where Jesus died so we might be free. Now it doesn't matter what I think, no, you won't find eternity here. Need to slow down and breathe. Snowbird, but no snow. The ashtray is full. The dead have yet to be discovered, but hear everything you do. I've got a bulletproof water bottle, and my mind's made up to leave the bed unmade. I'll eat an apple while there's still an apple to eat. It's too late to quit this cigarette. All that's left to find is on the page, one last cup after this one. Vanity in every SUV you drive. I've got my black glass. And your last line will be filled with apologies.

Maria plays soccer; her grandfather, word games. Jess knew the truth but couldn't say it. I scratch my back on the back of my chair. God is grapefruit. She's banging something upstairs with a hammer. Wing-tipped creatures at my feet. I've got everything here you need, but I'm too late. Maria scored twice; Jack never looked up from his crossword puzzle. There's a foreboding newscast behind the violins. "Catastrophic," it's the only audible word; it fits both down and across. Jack was dumbfounded. (pause) Made a few phone calls just to hear a human voice. Could move to Idaho maybe Iceland. And the wind chimes and the light goes out. All my clocks have fallen back, but time is irrelevant if you're not counting. Jess's busy making trinkets for the holiday season, flaming hearts, rings, mother and daughter pendants, bracelets, earrings. I need a whistle for my chain, a wind to supplement the air I breathe. I will not count the time. Above the line there are no puppets that dangle from telephone wire. No rotting posts. No village is home, and home is no place. I can see her bedroom window from here if I stand on a footstool and lean to the left. Curtains of lace. A warm, soft, shadowy grace moves in silhouette, black tears embroidered on black glass. I am reason enough to believe, and where it ends, I stop.

*   *   *

Don't know what page I'm on. How to fit myself inside this box. It's a desolate Sunday afternoon; we sit in the sun behind the picture window's glass and filter through the dust particles. It's a lonely place, these words on a page. No one calls, my hair's on edge like an electrical storm. I've got my coffee, cigarettes, and sugar-free cough drops, some good music to kill the silence. Not such a bad mess that I can't clean it up, put it on the page where no man hides. (later) Ate something, but that was yesterday. I'm feeling more dead than alive. Tim hands me a tissue as if it were the right hand of God; we exchange horse whispers, gobs into the bucket, his from the tube in his throat, mine from my nose. (pause) Ms. Ladybug lands on the page, curtseys twice and flies off. The music stops. This chapter ends.

*　　　*　　　*

Chapter 9

last train out

...and the doors on the street are shut as the sound of the grinding mill is low, and one will arise at the sound of the bird, and all the daughters of song will sing softly. Eccl. 12:4

*   *   *

Don't know how I got here, how anyone arrives. Waiting on a bird, a train whistle, a voice. To do more than just bounce on and off the black glass. It's me who sleeps with a light on these days, shot through them cracks like a prison break. Woke up screeching, silenced, before the cough, caught in a mouthful of knots that couldn't come unglued. I know how it ends, but I don't know how to stop it. Shay Full of Grace just sits there and remembers nothing. I pull words from a hat and put it on my head. I kill one lamp, I only need one. The ashtray was full a long time ago; it will never be empty again. Again just to fill the page like a wisp of blue ribbon for your hair. And this too is vanity.

Mildred's invited me to Maria's soccer game, her team's playing for the state championship. Big Charlie also called; he's gonna be out of town caring for his mom who's real sick with the flu. Big Charlie hates Jack, tolerates Mildred, thinks the family's one big, sick masquerade ball.

Everyone knows what nobody talks about. Feels better if someone's got an eye on Jack. (pause) Above the line it's different, silence rings true, there are no sugary substitutes. I need one more cup to start the ashtray over again. And the page fills its lonesome self. The light will come sooner now, now that clocks have been changed. I like it here, just God, me, an empty page. I'll clean myself up, walk my way to the meeting under the sparrow tree, past the inn where she stayed, take my seat on the church steps, wave hello and goodbye to the Newsman. I will step down into the basement; listen to the rhetoric over, over and again, and again to break the wisdom of fools with a small, simple, but vibrant package of verse. It's all been arranged, it's already happened. They might have to cut my neck open again, but they won't find me there, won't let 'em take away my voice. See, I'm here on the page. This is the seat where I listen best, these circular moves I can fit myself inside of. Here come the birds unseen but heard, out from the black glass. Again that train whistles off in the distance, down by the river, but you can't swim there no more. (pause) Above the line you can eat the fish, and swim like the fishes do. This train goes on forever it seems, recast in bronze like Daddy's first pair of baby shoes. Yeah, maybe, but this is the last train out. Ed's dead on the block from a flurry of pokes, shocks to the brain. Another good soldier gone to heaven, delivered up from the fury of Hell. Yeah, life ain't fair. There are no footprints in the sand, no blue sand castles, beach heads, no sunbathing allowed. The sun's too damn hot anymore, even the ocean's on fire. What was it Abraham told Isaac? "Son, this ain't no oil slick burning, its blood!"

We turn the page. (pause) Take our pills. Still, this metal taste in my mouth. Pssst! Let the day reveal itself. While shaving I found another lump on the opposite side of my throat, it was a year ago they cut out the first one. I'd like to finish this book, all else is vanity. Even to finish is to die, matters little. It's only out of necessity I write, killing time like shooting stars and empty bottles, like postcards off the window's ledge. The back wood is getting naked; soon all will be a tangle of sticks. I will walk my way front and back, and into the black glass. There will be no moon, no stars, no reason, just, just because. All these bottles are made of plastic anymore, ever since the milk truck's been replaced. No sparrows in the sparrow tree, no wedding rice, sidewalk's just a sea of dead leaves. Saw a red tree burning in the sunlight, pure like the voice of God. An old woman wrinkled by time made her way up the path, bathrobe and walking cane. She spoke in a soft voice unaffected by her age. I retrieved her newspaper off the curb, handed it over. "You won't find any truth in there."

"I know, its smut. I need the coupons." She smiled, blessed my day like a guardian angel. This church step, it's cold; it's even colder in the basement these days. (later) There was a dream. I was in the dressing room following the performance, waiting to meet God. He called himself Henry Miller but looked like Bob Dylan, wanted me to play ping-pong. Jess was in the dream; she looked good, alive, and so beautiful; we were made to sit on opposite sides of the room. The stage manager wanted me to sign on as a roadie. "I'm a writer, I don't need a job."

"God wants to write your book."

I'd nothing left to think about, didn't hesitate, "Sure," I signed on for the tour. In the end God let me win at ping-pong. (pause) I'm sad with no reprieve in sight. There's snow in the forecast and too many leaves on the trees. Might we all break apart? I helped someone I don't like complete a poem. It made for better relations. I look forward to seeing my fellow Horsemen each day, each waits on another waiting his turn. I push Tim's wheelchair, he keeps me in tissues. They're gonna cut some cancer off the top of my ear. (long pause) That piece ain't comin' back like some of these lumps ain't goin' away. The flesh bows and the music soars. I need to hole up and finish this book. I need to eat something that slides down. I still make the bed, and still the light goes out. Me, Tim, and Rene, we ain't afraid of dying, and John, he recently joined our group, they took his voice, put a permanent hole in his throat. Phil's not missing that foot any, helped me get through a difficult night.

I gagged on that last sip. Put my hand to my ear, forgot it was stitched. It came out my noise. There's no second wind after this one. No page but the one I'm on. I'm running out of lives, but I think I've got it right. Who's counting? No, you're mistaken. Yeah, I saw Jimmy Cagney in *Angels with Dirty Faces*, face, it's a great word, always gets your attention, but it's been abused. I won't be fine; I can feel it in the bones of my face. No, I don't think I'll miss myself any. Tried calling Shay, I can tell her anything and she won't tell Mom. (pause) A nurse answered, seems Shay Full of Grace died in her sleep, suffocated in a pillow of dream at the right hand of God.

*   *   *

Rain. Slept late. That was yesterday. Now it seems I need almost no sleep, like I'm pressed between the page and where it stops. The glass is clear but teary eyed. Gray is the color. I see the cancer doctor today, but I'm not feeling optimistic. Don't remember any dreams. No walk or meeting this morning, just this metal paste in my throat. I need to talk to someone outside the glass, who knows what I'm doing in here, inside-out on a black screen. Think Tim is next in line, his roommate Mr. Lindsey died last night. Tim agrees, this here is worse than War, everybody dies. All this treatment hasn't made me any better. There are birds but none in view; still, I can see them with my eyes closed. There's a grist mill down that slope. What is it? What don't you get? Yeah, I'm insecure in sackcloth, trying to be nice, but there's nothing to figure out. It doesn't matter where it came from, cigarettes or orange smoke. It might have been the milk, the drinking water, that last sip. (later) Two biopsies, my ear and my throat. What you already know. God, I need some help here. A small nap, no phone calls. One out in the ashtray and the bases are empty. Just get me off this page; it's the bottom of the last cup. They've given me another pill to take. Think I need a walk. The baby wrens return all grown up. The lamp I thought was broken works. The bed, the coffee pot, the ashtray. The rain has stopped. Red bird feeding on my pretzel crumbs. Seems there are only skeletal fingers with skeleton keys bolting for doorways. Don't know who to ask, like I've gotta to do this all alone. I'm cold for no reason. (pause) Can't get anyone on the phone. It's just God, me, and them bones. Still waiting on someone, I don't know who, like I'm stuck someplace I've been before and need to get out from between. Need to get off this split-screen effect, page and glass, the rise and fall of ocean floors, life after War time, *Oh them bones, them bones, them skeleton bones*! I'd like to be a white linen handkerchief on the mast of a tall sail ship. I'm sadder than the story reveals. You can see it in my walk, in the crumpling of paper sheets, how the blood coagulates.

*   *   *

Black glass. Black cough. What's lost and found me in the Valley of Dry Bones, somewhere between the first lines of page and the need to start over again. And the story's never told but keeps moving as planned. It's just me and Tim at this hour, like I've written this before. Before the birds, the song, before there were bills to pay, before we got sick. 4 hours before daylight. I've got enough coffee and cigarettes to finish this book. Had more than enough pain that it can't stop me anymore. I turn the page. I've no enthusiasm, no time for success, no buttons left on this red cowboy shirt. My blue house, I can't remember how it looks, how I lost it, that the window was left open and the rains came in. Jill kicked the bucket; Jack fell down and broke his crown. That postcard like the wallpaper you'd pin the tail on the donkey with, it's wrinkled, smeared, warped, all watered down, I'm all disfigured now. (pause) Above the line the page is like a lamb to pasture; down the line is great pain and long suffering. Life's like a slaughterhouse with a moonroof, save your prayers, give me your time, a timely read. At this moment the words are winning. God is having his way with me. And the wind chimes 3 beats, past, present, and no future. Yeah, we're all here, the living, the dead and the dying. I've got no foothold on any of this, no mountain view, but a bucket full of nothin'. (pause) Jess had an affair with a married man; he'd promised her everything but left her broken in the end. Big Charlie almost killed the guy, threw a tantrum on his front lawn, let his wife and all his neighbors hear 'im, shot his dog. It's getting harder to drink this fucking paste; I've got blisters on my tongue screaming out with every sip. There's that train whistle again barking out the night, a memory like a jackhammer chisels at my brain, vibrates along my entire failing body and aching joints like a series of speed bumps. (pause) That affair cost Jess her marriage, left her desperately alone and landed her in a psych hospital. Since her divorce all her choices have been bad ones, unavailable men, or overly dependent immature bums, assholes! "I guess I got a bad picker," she jokes, but it's herself she hates. She'd been trying to believe she deserves something better, not rushing into things, spending more time with Maria. Me, I'm not fooling anyone, I know my limitations, my unavailability. Truth is, I'm dying. Those are my footsteps on the ceiling; I'm making handprints in cement. Yes, I can, I must finish. They've increased my pain meds, but it hasn't lessened the pain any, nodded out at the urinal, woke up in the smoke room with my PJs on fire. The light's shooting up like chariots ablaze, come to rescue me from the radio that plays through the air ducts, the slap, slapping of tire tread flapping off the roadway, the sound of metal locusts ringing in my ear. There are certain things I'll miss, but so much is already missing. No, I haven't any children, no Jess, no blue house, no fast car I'm driving, hey, that's a piece of my ear in your alphabet soup. (pause) No, I'm not dead yet, no matter how many times I've already died. Stop! Hey God, might I even survive this? I need a clean washcloth, a bowl for my oatmeal, a snowy jaunt with Harold, once, twice around the block. (pause)

Dead poets tied to a red tree, just how the light hits the leaves. That's the inn where she slept, she gave me this tea, and it's soft, gentle on my throat. "Go right at the next light, and the train station's up about 3 miles on the left, can't miss it." It's a cold church step; I share it with a dead leaf. Slept for an hour, just a nod, last night only 3, all this pain keeps me awake. None of it matters much. 14 pill bottles, 3 swishers, one to swallow, one paste shake, did 4 cans yesterday. I'm a small knot on a tight rope. (pause) Some sleep, a dry shirt. I'll miss the turning of the page, black glass into morning light. Won't miss the traffic any, picking lint off the living room carpet, leaf blowing, babies crying. (pause) One can consumed. I do love the words. Won't miss my dying pain, most of the people here, but the morning meeting, the walk, what seasonal changes, autumn's colors, spring's renewal, winter's moon. I'd like to know how long I've got, put my house in order, say goodbye to all my friends, the ones I'm gonna miss. I will not rage, but embrace the dying of the light. I will not endure needless suffering. Having died so many times before I'll know when to jump, shoot first, die with my boots on and a smile on my face. (pause) Two pain pills and a can of paste. I'm not feeling forsaken, not like Jesus, Mother Teresa or a wounded soldier pinned down in a crossfire, nailed to them floorboards. I'll know when it's my time.

Longevity is an egg timer wrong-side up. I won't have another tooth pulled, or fill another cavity. I will not melt in the sun, or freeze in the shadows. I will not measure out my life in coffee spoons, count the pages, how many cups, but I will fill you up. Ask me, what's next? (later) Not much of a nap, this time or that. You're not here, on either side of it. One message from Jess, left her one back but didn't say much, only the good stuff. Know enough about death to know the hardest thing there is, is being left behind. Motherfucker! Now it's my turn! No more pieces, bits, no pick-up sticks, and this little bullet hole went straight through to China. Keep thinking I've been here before, and not just with a pen. My name's not Lazarus now, but more like Humpty Dumpty. Soon I won't have to make the bed; there'll be no shoes to shine or mountains to move. You'll be leaving me phone messages, but I won't return your calls. You'll pray, but no one will answer your prayers. You'll wish you were dead, but will only have to wait your turn. (pause) It's me who's next!

(pause) I can manage the pain from here, a blue and a red pill. It's all about pain management. No more waiting on lines at the supermarket, lines at the gas pumps, pharmacy lines. No more blue lines on a blank page, "fill 'er up," no shopping bags to carry, no more up and down escalators. Won't need any bees to pollinate my ass, no solar energy to warm my bones. (pause) Me and Shay would dig holes in the dirt, race each other to China. Mom said, "There're children over there starving to death." So we mailed them our lima beans. At least we tried to, but Mom wouldn't let us. Now Shay's cooking up all them lima beans for God to eat. (pause) Got a box of blank checks in the mail, more than I'll need to write. It's that sinking time of day. A cold sip of paste just burped out my nose. It's snowing, looks like a postcard you'd bring down from the mountain, home to your grandkids. Where's my friend Harold? Tim's all wrinkled, pale, laugh lines yellowed, exhausted, a young man in a dead man's suit. "Can't sleep with this tube in my throat," he's afraid he'll choke on it.

Had Jess known how sick I'd be, she never would have left me here. Who to tell? What I don't know for sure, but surely know. No, not until I know for certain, still, no one knows nothin' but God. You might step off that street corner and get drilled by a milk wagon. The hardest thing left for me to do is to say goodbye and leave you crying. And the wind chimes a metallic lullaby while the lion sleeps tonight in my dreams. This is my gift to you, my gift from God.

There were two therapists who tried to take advantage of Jess. I don't pretend to know all the wherefores, the reasons why, how this happens, just that it's fucked up. It seems a victim broadcasts his or herself as if on a sandwich board, an easy score, weak, vulnerable, needy, an innate sensitivity to be abused. Just ask the Big Man. A perp's like a wolf, can smell a meal from miles away, knows if your weak, what to say, how to proceed and when to strike. Jess's Aunt Molly had died, she was like a mom, was there for her in ways Mildred never could be. Jess couldn't stop crying, sobbing, out of control. Dr. Bentway got up from his office chair, out from behind his desk and sat beside her on the couch, put his arm around her shoulder, "Its okay darling, it's all gonna be okay." She was crying so, that she couldn't speak. He unbuttoned her blouse, jumped her bones. (pause) Called home. I substituted silence for truth, until I know for certain. My mom asks too many questions. "You get 3 from now on, and no more."

"Why only 3?"

"That's one too many."

Again it's that time of day when everything sinks. Again I only want out. Out from the noise, this darkness. It's an overwhelmingly sad song. Everything's broken and there's no time to do the work. I only feel bad. Where's Myles? Where's Ed, Shay, Jess? What's too early, you're too late for. We need more sleep. I make the bed both then and now, and it makes no difference, the distance is the same. It won't put an end to any of this. Who's leaving? Who's back from the dead? I've got a mouth full of metal, and I'm peeling like a sunburn screams, chariots afire, jumping through hoops, like the back of my neck's been hit with a blowtorch. Elijah's coming. Please, take me up! (pause) The phone rings but no one's there, comes up unavailable. I want to shoot the works and the sins of the father. I want to rise up above the dead, far from my dying self. A child runs off ahead of her mom, her mother calling out after her, "Jess, Jessica, wait for me!" I grab the girl's belt jacket from behind and jerk her back onto the sidewalk, out of the street, out from in front of a passing truck, out from her mother's worst nightmare. And the music stops. (pause) It's all there is to be done about it? Turn the page; pile your dead over there. Because, it's my job. Seems you can't make any friends sayin' you were raped. If you volunteer any information, someone will gladly screw you. And when you're dead and in the ground someone will dig you up and fuck your bones! I have no lover, no aspirations about falling in love. There's no wedding rice, that's bird shit. Empty, rinse, clear, tray, cup, ashes, ashes, ashes! I don't need your prayers. I don't want your time. Shay's waiting.

Much too early for song, just one step ahead of the pain, out from the black glass and onto the page. Not that many more pages, but too many bullet holes to patch. There's that train whistle, down by the river. (pause) My mother called, she needs to stop all the questions. All I need to do is wave.

* * *

We were standing on the platform waiting on a train. It was late, it was the last train out until morning, and it was late in coming. The station was almost empty but for a few small groups of persons scattered about. Jack walked off to find a paper and a bathroom. Mildred, Maria, and myself stood about, making pleasant conversation. "You were terrific!"

Mildred agrees, "You were magnificent, my dear." Maria's team had won the game and were now state champs. We were all in good spirits. Maria had scored the tie-breaking goal with only seconds remaining on the clock. Just 14, only a sophomore, she was now the envy of every high school debutant. Unlike her mom, Maria Full of Grace was shy, quiet, soft-spoken; but they were both strikingly beautiful, possessed a wallop of a kick! We were laughing about the time Big Charlie put me flat out on my back and broke my nose. There were a slew of rats below racing between the rails; sifting through the garbage strewn about. A McDonald's bag was being torn apart, its contents devoured, what was left of a hamburger, some fries, and a sesame seed bun. If Jess were here she'd have something funny to say. (pause) If! Why does all this feel so strangely familiar? Was it a movie or a dream? Those dreams when you know you're dreaming, you're enjoying yourself, and don't ever wanna wake up. Seems we walk in and out of dream, changing places, names, arranging and rearranging the furniture. (pause) Her naked window needs new curtains. Walked under the red tree, stole a leaf for my kitchen vase. Came inside, it's too cold for steps, cold enough that what leaves are left on the trees should fall to the ground. My mom, my brother Billy, and my sister Marianne are coming to see me. No Shay, she's gone. I hope Bill brings his boys, Brett and Chris. This might be where we say goodbye, what I feel, but only God knows for certain. Maria Full of Grace looks like her mom, and Jess like Mildred, 3 generations unfurled. I see them all as one reflected off the yellow ceramic tile of this filthy train station. Above the line and rat piss I can smell marigolds. I'm just a pill above the pain. It's hard to focus Mr.

Jones, and my speaking voice, it comes and goes like the turning of a page. (later) They don't want to know I'm dying, I can't help knowing. I was hoarse from cheering. Maria Full of Grace gets quiet, withdrawn, reserved for a girl who's just won the state finials with a tie-breaking goal. She looked sad almost, tired perhaps after all the day's excitement. "I wish my mom were here." Mildred was the first to respond, "Yes, so do I dear, she'd be so proud of you." (pause)

No good dreams but for skipping stones across a frozen lake, stones big enough to break the ice. I need a phone call, a gusty blast of wind, the page to set itself straight. The trash is out; the mail is in, nothing worth opening, no phone messages. I'm pumping coffee, puffing down a cigarette. Again I'm starting over, what's almost over. Bullet holes and no treaties to sign. Above the line you can see forever. "Here Brett, you take these milk bottles, and run up that walk!" (pause) My feet are cold and I've no socks without holes. I'm leaving the bed the way it is, like a cold and sweaty nightmare; it's a good day to stick it all behind the warm glass. This is the winter of my truth. Yeah, it looks like snow, like they've caught me here on time. (pause) The patio is swept. I've got enough cigarettes to finish this. Still, this hollow, empty Christmas stocking feeling. The bed's made because, on account of, it's my job. Not a good night's sleep, up and down, and up all night but mostly coughing myself awake. And the pain. There are no dreams I haven't spit up. This sunburn's raw, oozes out yellow puss and wakes me stuck to the pillow.

I just had to say something to Maria, she needed to know about Jack, how he'd traumatized her mother's life, repeatedly compromised her wellbeing, why she cut herself again, over and again and just couldn't get out from under. She needed to know the truth, feel protected, validated, and comfortable in her own skin. And the wind chimes luxuriously, what's simple and sure of itself. I'm a good scribe, back on the page where I belong. Mildred's busy pacing like a rubber ball in a concrete breezeway, "Where the hell is he? We'll miss our train."

"We'll leave without him."

Mildred laughs, "I should be so lucky. You didn't hear that, Maria." Some kids at the far end of the station were getting loud, music blasting, laughing and hurling obscenities, tossing empty beer cans at each other and onto the tracks. They were too far off to matter, make a difference, be of any threat. "Maria, (pause) your grandfather, (pause) he sexually abused your mother." Mildred jumps as if sprung from a trampoline, "Stop! Don't tell her such things."

"It's the truth Mildred, she needs to know."

"No, she doesn't!"

"Yes, Mildred, you should tell her."

"No, I won't!"

"Stop it, both of you!" Maria gets all watery eyed, "You're like children." She's about to implode like the solitary shrill of a field mouse laid bare to the hawk. "I already know." She weeps quietly to herself.

"What? What did you say?" Mildred moves to put her arm around Maria, "Its okay, darling." Maria pulls away, steps back into herself.

"No, it's not okay! I told my mom just 3 weeks before she died that Grandpa had been giving me drinks, getting me drunk, touching me where he shouldn't, making me promise not to tell. After that my mom got depressed, wouldn't get out of bed, started drinking again." A train whistle roars out like a famished lion come out from his jungle lair, out for the hunt. And here comes Jack down the ramp, a big fat smile on his face, waving his newspaper,

"Here comes the train everybody!" Mildred's crying, shuffles her feet, wipes away the tears. She whispers something to Maria; they embrace, lock themselves up tight in each other's arms.

*   *   *

Here it's silent, but for a few lonely wind chimes, nothing like a train and the excitement it creates. 3 beats, 3 butts in the ashtray. Tim's got 4 teeth, two less than me. He's getting worse, now like John they're gonna take away his voice. Now it's Bucky, a recently enlisted Horseman, or me, who's next on deck to be silenced. You can't take away the page! The back wood's coming into view. A car alarm sounds like a train roaring off track. Jack sees Mildred comforting Maria, sees she's been crying, "What's wrong with my little tootsie pop?" That's it, that was my last sip. I dare not drink another cup of you! Above the line there are no perpetrators, I've killed them all! There are no consequences here, not if you're already dying of cancer. (pause) A walk among the dead leaves, like Jesus walked on water. No sparrows. No red tree. No tall sail ship a-sailing. Just bones anymore like wavering sticks in muddy waters. Been here almost 5 weeks already, with not much further to tell. I'm sad and with no other recourse, pissed, ain't nothin' else to be done about it. I grabbed Jack by his belt, bent my knees, arched my back, spun him around and about like a spinning top, spun him out, let him go and onto the tracks. Splat! Splat goes Jack like a hammered bug. And all the train whistles of the world scream out as one, like Moses come down from the mountain with a slab of rock. The word of God! Breaks and heartbeats screeching to a halt, squealing like a burst pig, a pureed Jack spraying out in all directions. A rat's feast come home to roost, better than a Big Mac. (pause) Two cops come out of nowhere like a bad western, slap the cuffs on me, behind my back. Mildred and Maria try to explain, but the cops know what they saw, I won't even deny it. "Yeah, I wanted him dead!" They read me my rights. I don't need any. I'll die before I'm prosecuted. All that's good is Jack is dead. All that matters is Maria's safe. "It's ain't your fault, kid."

(later) A nice nap, uninterrupted sleep. The sun's shining through the back wood like the only truth I know. In my dream I wore a new coat, its lining double stitched. Two phone messages, no mail. I need to make the bed one last time. Need to tell Jess she can come back here now, there's no need to cut and run, the way has been cleared. Rene doesn't have to die here. Tim and Bucky are planning a road trip. John needs to learn how to read and write and sign. Phil's gonna plant a garden, tomatoes, onions, Brussels sprouts, basil, get down there in the dirt and dig straight through to China. Send Shay all them lima beans; she'll cook 'em up good! Me, I'm just a scribe; this just might be my last page. Above the line there's no orange smoke, and everybody's stopped smoking. Killing Jack was what I wanted to do but didn't, Mildred knew better. She called two cops over who just happened to be there at the right time passing. She had Jack arrested, she told the cops what Jack had done. How he'd molested their daughter, and now her granddaughter. Maria's testimony convinced 'em, "It's over, Grandpa, I hate you!" The cops slapped the cuffs on Jack, real tight, read him his rights. They took him away sniveling like a little brat of a schoolboy, a bully gone soft. After all these years Mildred had stopped doing nothin', and did something about it. She felt good, real good about herself. It was all good. Mildred, Maria, and I do believe Jess was there, they boarded the last train out. (pause) Me, I'm waving goodbye. And the wind chimes. My cup is empty, the music stops. My cigarette falls from my hand to the page. All this before that hillside had ever been imagined.

* * *

Acknowledgments

*   *   *

I would like to thank Lauren Manoy, Nancy Kelly Weimer, Larry Winters, Dayl Wise, Bonnie Nasca, Ann Bogart, Barbara Klar for Clear Metals, Faith Payne (art works), Branda Miller, Rich Gaz, Gary Wogisch, Phillip Levine and Robert Long, thank you.

And thank you Jess.

*   *   *

Printed in the United States
206347BV00007B/1-39/P